Midnight Hour

Second in the Until Dawn Series

Midnight Hour

Second in the Until Dawn Series

By J. Elaine Knight

Midnight Hour
Second in the Until Dawn Series

Paperback: (979-8-950072-32-1)
Hardcover: (979-8-950072-33-8)

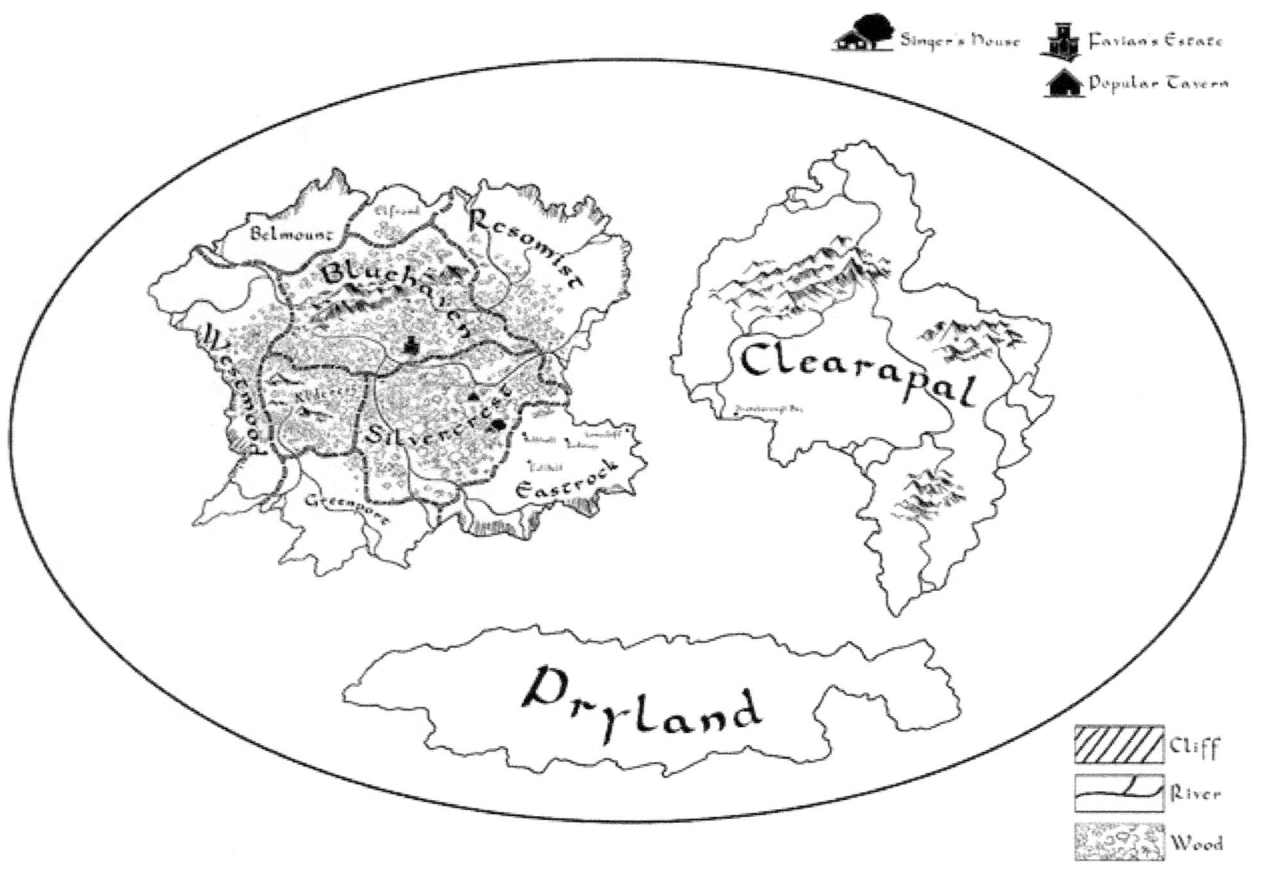
Singer's House
Favian's Estate
Popular Tavern
Belmount
Resomist
Bluehaven
Westmood
Silvercrest
Eastrock
Greenport
Clearapal
Dryland
Cliff
River
Wood

In the midnight hour,

See me safely through the night.

I

Silence. Sweet, sweet silence. No whistling wind, no animals clamoring in the surrounding trees- just blissful stillness. A sigh left my lips as I closed my eyes, allowing the hush of the night to consume me. When was the last time I had such a peaceful dream?

"Haven't you learned?" Fear strangled me until a cold numbness paralyzed my limbs.

"No..." I could barely hear the leaves crunching under heavy footfalls over my pounding heart. My mind scrambled, thoughts running a million miles a second.

"Just like your family," A twig snap. "You can't escape!" With a hitch in my breath, I bolted, running anywhere that was away from the man chasing me- the *murderer.*

How can he follow me here? Why is he always in my dreams?!

What was the point in running anymore? The faster I ran, the quicker his steps became. The further I think I get away, the closer he becomes. Tears blinded my vision as I sucked in a breath.

Just as my legs were about to give out, a light shined brightly before me, a welcoming warmth radiating through it. With a blast of energy, my feet lurched forward, my mind finally focused on one goal-

Reach sanctuary!

"It's quite simple actually, I want the jewel that my former employer has asked for." My blood ran cold as realization dawned.

No! This can't be happening!

I screamed- *begged* my feet to stop. They need to- they *have* to!

I don't want to die again! I can't take it!

"No! You can't have it!" The sound of my own voice screaming but not coming from my lips terrified me.

Please- not again!

“But,” I gasped as I ran straight into the blinding light. Squeezing my eyes shut, the world fell silent. My feet *finally* stilled, letting me catch my breath. Once the light faded, I opened my eyes. The moment everything came into focus, my blood turned to ice.

Bellatrix sat on her throne, watching the scene before her in mild interest. Layne lay face down in a pool of his own blood with a handkerchief stained red, thrown on top of his body like trash. Hawk stood over him, a gun in his hand aimed straight at me, and Singer right behind him, frozen in a lunge.

“It’s my wish.” A deafening bang. Searing pain and then a hollow darkness...

***

“No-!” I covered my mouth quickly.

I panted frantically looking around. When it clicked, I was alone, a shaky exhale left my lips. Dropping my head, I allowed the first few tears to fall before gently whipping them away.

“I’m so tired.” I sighed before a sharp pain made me wince.

Tossing the blankets aside, I threw my legs over the edge of the bed.

Sucking in a deep breath, I pulled up my shirt enough to see the wound Hawk gave me that day. A nasty pink scar slowly disappearing met my gaze on the right side of my stomach. I can feel the blood pumping beneath it making it sting. Hesitantly, I lightly grazed it with a finger. A faint burning sensation emanated before it gradually ebbed away. Sighing, I dropped my shirt.

“It could be worse.” I whisper to myself.

Placing both hands on the bed, I slowly pushed myself onto my feet. The still healing skin stretched and burned. A pained squeak flew out my lips as I paused. Once the pain faded, I let out a relieved huff.

But this sucks.

Straightening, my eyes automatically landed on the flower bud resting on the bedside table. A flash of Aric’s boyish smile made my heart lurch violently. What happens when he becomes a fairy? Will he remember me? Will he still be a boy or a man? Will we be able to stay together?

What if he never wakes up?

Shaking my head, I shoved that dark thought from my mind. Aric *will* wake up. Aric will become a fairy and I'll take care of him like always.

Everything will be fine.

Reaching out, I grabbed the flower and tucked it away in my skirt pocket. Keeping my hand protectively over the bud, I slowly hobbled to the door.

Peeking into the hallway, I scanned for signs of Lilly. When I didn't see her, I stepped out and walked down the hall. Light poured in through the roof creating rays that gradually illuminated my path. By the time I made it to the foyer, the room was bathed in fresh sunlight. Keeping my body carefully hidden behind the wall, I peeped over the railing. When I still didn't see Lilly, my body relaxed.

No one's home. Finally!

Whirling around, I made my way to the front door. Just the thought of being outside made me salivate.

I've been in here for way too-

My breath hitched as my key to freedom swung open revealing Lilly. A hand-woven basket filled with fruits and an assortment of flowers was tucked neatly under her arm. The moment our eyes met, I knew any chances of making it out these stifling walls were gone.

I must be blessed with divine timing.

"Jayde? What are you doing out of bed?" her eyes slowly narrowed as they scanned me from head to toe. I tried not to look bothered, but internally, I was ripping my hair out.

Yep- truly blessed.

"Well," lowering my gaze, I put on my best doe eyes, "it's been two weeks since I tried walking-"

"And four since you were shot!" She howled, dropping her basket. Placing her hands on my shoulders, she turned me around and pushed me down the hall. "You're human, Jayde. You need a *lot* more than a month to recover!"

Here we go again.

Groaning, I tore my shoulders from her grasp and faced her.

"Can't you just - I don't know- sprinkle more healing magic on it?"

"I've already used too much! Who knows the repercussions it could have on your body? Besides, why are you so desperate to leave?" She leaned closer, her intense pink eyes making me shrink. "Are you trying to run off on that suicide mission to Clearapal?" I scoffed, crossing my arms.

"Maybe," Her features darkened. "Or maybe I want to see someone?" Immediately, a cheesy grin stretched her lips as a halo of light encompassed her.

"If you wanted to spend time with your future husband, you should've just said so! He's out back with his father and the twins." With a dramatic gasp, she latched onto my shoulders. The sparks in her eyes blinded me. "If you go now you can surprise him!"

Snatching my arm, she started dragging me down the hall towards the stairs.

Why does she always do this when I mention Singer?

Now that I think about it, Lilly has done this ever since I met her. Call me crazy, but I don't think she would just randomly accept me out of the blue- no matter how cute she thinks I am.

"Ms. Lilly," I stopped at the top of the stairs, pulling back on her gently. She looked back at me in concern.

"What's wrong Jayde? Did I hurt you?" I shook my head, trying to find the right words.

"Why do you like me so much? I mean, why do you keep pushing me and Singer to be together?" She blinked for a moment like she didn't understand what I was saying. After a few seconds, the corners of her mouth slightly downturned as a distant fog covered her eyes that made my heart clench.

"You... remind me of someone I knew a long time ago. Someone I should've done more for." I wanted to ask her more, but the lump in my throat wouldn't let me.

Seeing her like this… doesn't feel right.

Whatever was going through her mind didn't last long. Her usually bright smile lit up her features as she gently tugged on my arm.

"Let's go before we miss Singer." Just like that, she resumed dragging down the stairs and to the back door. Without pausing, she swung it open, revealing the rest of the family.

Even though the house is a fairly average size, the backyard is humongous. About an acre was cleared for a spacious flatland. Most of it was empty leaving ample space for sparring. A medium sized tree off to the right had two swings and a tight rope hanging from the limbs. Next to it was a larger tree with a modest treehouse hidden in its branches. A wooden walkway within the canopy connected the two. The surrounding forestry outlined the edges of the boundary just before a steep drop off.

Singer and Anar faced off in the center of the clearing. The twins sat on the swings watching the older males intensely. Lilly waved excitedly, dragging me behind her.

"Singer! Your future wife came to visit you!" She bellowed.

Said boy turned his head with a lit scowl.

"Mother, I'm in the middle of a-" Anar lunged at him wielding a staff made out of a glistening obsidian metal before he could finish.

Singer dodged by a hair only for his feet to be swept from beneath him. He hit the ground hard. Anar jumped on top of him. He swung his staff down only to hit air when Singer's body evaporated. Anar stood, his eyes scanning the area. Suddenly, he swung his staff in a fluid arch behind him at nothing. His brows pinched for a moment before he straightened.

"More illusions?" He closed his eyes, lifting his left arm across his body, his palm parallel to the ground. "Break." He firmly stated, his eyes snapped open as Singer appeared out of nowhere from the ground. Singer aimed a kick at Anar's midsection, but the older of the two was faster. As Anar blocked it with his staff, a smirk appeared on Singer's face.

"You still fall for them, old man." Singer evaporated into thin air. Anar's eyes widened a fraction as he jumped back, but before he could get away, tree roots shot from the ground wrapping around the expanse of his body until they entrapped him. Anar struggled until a sigh broke through his lips.

"Fine- you win this time, boy." The ground in front of Anar cracked open as Singer slowly emerged seated on a throne of roots.

The smug smirk he sported only made him look more cocky.

"This makes my 105 to your 107." Anar chuckled, flexing his fingers. In the next second, the roots turned to ash releasing him. As Anar rubbed his wrists, the arrogant air surrounding Singer melted into an annoyed frown.

"I know. You're beginning to catch up to me which means you're getting better at keeping your repulsive personality from getting the better of you. Isn't that right, young Jayde?" I blinked, surprised he was acknowledging me before giving Singer a once-over.

"He might be getting a *little* better at fighting, but his personality definitely isn't any better. He's still way too reckless."

Singer scoffed, folding his arms.

"Really? Name one example."

"What about the time you let Layne shoot you?"

"That was completely necessary. Do you even know what an interrogation looks like?"

"The interrogator doesn't usually get shot."

"But he told me everything."

"Point made- you're reckless."

"And you're incompetent, stray." The air surrounding us chilled as we stared each other down, not willing to yield to the other. A moment passed before the patter of small feet broke off our glaring contest.

"You're all better!" Claribel shouted,wrapping her arms around me. Her head hit my wound, making me wince. Taking a breath, I returned her hug with a small smile.

"Better than yesterday. Thank you for worrying about me."

Claribel beamed as she took a step back.

"I knew you'd be ok. Mommy can heal anything!" A sly smirk fell on her lips as she leaned in. "But Singer was so worried, he wouldn't leave mommy alone." A resounding smack was heard.

Claribel held her head in pain as she glared up at Singer. "That hurt!"

"Don't spread nonsense and there won't be consequences."

The young girl pouted some more as she ran over to Lilly wailing that Singer was a 'big meanie'. Lilly chuckled, motioning for Claribel, Eallair, and Anar to go inside.

"Come on, let's give the two some time to talk! After all, Singer's future wife just got better." I rolled my eyes.

Seriously, what is with this woman and her obsession with her son's love life?

"Don't hold your breath."

"Never say never, sweetheart." She hummed as Clairbel, Eallair, and Anar disappeared inside.

"He's the one that says it."

"Nonsense." Lilly waved her hand in a dismissive gesture, that girlish grin never wavering.

"It's true - I loathe her presence." Lilly shot Singer a nasty glare that made the repulsive fairy shiver. Satisfied, her face softened as we locked eyes.

"Come in when you're ready." She gave me one last smile before leaving.

"You should go inside too." My brow raised as I looked over Singer's uninterested expression.

Where did that come from?

"Why?"

"Because you'd probably die from the *sharp* chill in the air." He nonchalantly stated. The slow smirk creeping on his lips made my eyes narrow.

"What- jealous it's sharper than your IQ?"

"That almost hurt."

"More or less than thinking of that comeback?"

"Less than it does being a walking bullseye. Even hobgoblins can see you're an easy target." He whirled around and crouched into a fighting stance before I could respond. I glared at his back as he started practicing punching combinations in the air.

What's his problem?

The more I watched him, the more I noticed the fluidity in his movements. Every twitch of his muscles, every miniscule motion he made was for a purpose. The longer I observed, the more things didn't make sense. Singer looks like he's been training for years. He's much faster than any human can dream of being. In that sense, shouldn't he have been able to prevent Hawk from shooting me? Shouldn't he have been fast enough to take the gun from Hawk before he had the chance to use it?
Then why did he attack Hawk when it was too late?

My eyes narrowed as I remembered that moment. I don't know what Singer was doing before Hawk pulled out the gun. The only time I can recall Singer doing anything was when Hawk pointed the barrel at me. Singer lunged just before he shot me, but why didn't he do anything beforehand?

Then again, why didn't Hawk kill me?

My eyes widened as realization dawned on me. If Hawk wanted me dead, why didn't he shoot to kill? He could've aimed for my head, heart- anywhere that would've guaranteed my death. If he truly wanted the jewel, why didn't he go for the kill? Did something stop him?

Did Singer save me?

"Back in the throne room," I called out to him. He paused, showing me that he was listening, "what were you doing before Hawk shot me?" He didn't even flinch as he switched to doing kick combinations.

"Well, while you were in the midst of your emotional outburst, I was trying to stop Hawk and his men. Keeping an army incapacitated isn't easy, stray." I stared at his back in astonishment.

"Then... what was that light I saw before I..." the words caught in my throat.

Just acknowledging the thought that I actually... that I actually *died* caused the memories- the *pain* to come back to the forefront of my mind. That hollow numbness quickly overshadowed by an unbearable, searing sensation. Singer's scoff brought me out of my musings as he kicked high in the air.

"Did you forget what a teleportation spell looks like, stray?"

The time we escaped from Layne.

I rolled my eyes.

"Must have slipped my mind after I got *shot*." Singer's body stiffened, but he still didn't face me.

"Oh good- *another* topic I'll never hear the end of."

Did he... did he really just say that?

Shock was quickly getting overrun with blinding rage. My teeth clenched tightly as I felt my nails digging painfully into my palms.

"Sorry my near death is an inconvenience for you to hear."

"You act as if it's a new thing."

"Then why did you save me?" I yelled, my eyes burning with angry tears. "If you'd let me die you wouldn't have to deal with any of this." He let out a frustrated grunt, whirling towards me with a fire burning behind his eyes.

"You're an idiot, stray."

"Then spell it out for me, *genius*." I spat.

"I made a promise to keep you safe and that's what I'm going to do!" he snarled, glaring at me.

Without saying another word, he turned on his heels and resumed his combinations. I scowled at his back as he punched and kicked the air in different combinations until something caught my attention.

His movements before held a purpose behind them. Now, some of his actions were pointless and held more power than needed.

Is he... frustrated?

The more I watched him, the more obvious it was.

What could I have said that made him so frustrated?

“Does it bother you that I was shot?” the words slipped from my mouth before I could even process them.

Singer faltered in his kick, knocking himself off balance. He caught himself returning to a standing position. Slowly, he turned, a scowl darkening his features.

“What makes you think something like that would bother me?” I shot him an exasperated look before turning my gaze off to the

distance.

“Well, you did say you promised to keep me safe and then I was shot so...” my voice trailed off. I glanced at him to gauge his reaction. He scoffed, crossing his arms across his chest.

“If you were in any real danger, Bellatrix would have blown that annoying rat back to whatever hole he crawled out of.”

“Why would she do that? Hawk and Layne both came with intentions to be granted a wish just like me.”

“You see? You make it very difficult for me to tolerate you with all of the nonsense that comes out of your mouth.” I glowered at him.

“Same to you. Now are you going to explain or continue to whine?” He rolled his eyes.

“Well it may have something to do with- I don’t know- the promise she made to Jaxon Henryk.”

“What does that have to do with anything? The only promise she made was to keep the jewel safe until a Henryk comes.”

“Maybe because you, being a Henryk and all, came to get the jewel and Hawk, being an assassin, came to take it.” I narrowed my eyes at his condescending tone. “Now, if you were to use some brain power here, you would see how allowing him to kill you would conflict with her promise.”

“I understand that much.” He scoffed at the pointed glare I sent his way. “What I don’t understand is why she would still care. Hasn’t it been, like, centuries since my ancestor lived?” an exaggerated sigh left his lips as he smacked his forehead.

“Idiot, a fairy is bound by their promises for life. It’s not like making a pinky promise with some other human and then breaking it in the next breath. These things are serious.” With that said, he whirled on his heel and resumed his punches.

A small smile found its way to my lips. A fairy is bound by their promises, huh? No wonder he’s been going out of his way to keep me safe. Well, *mostly* safe.

"Thank you." Again, he faltered in his formation nearly falling flat on his face. Once he caught himself, he slowly turned a suspicious eye to me.

"What possessed you to utter such blasphemy?" Rolling my eyes, my smile grew wider.

"Everything that you've done for me- the things I know about and the things I don't. I just want to say thank you, even though your whole 'I-don't-care' act won't allow you to accept it, I just wanted you to hear it." He stared at me for a heartbeat before his left eyebrow twitched. With a forced cough, he turned his back.

"Get inside before you catch a cold and die, you insufferable stray." A soft giggle left my lips as I turned to leave.

"You act like a little boy that doesn't want to admit he has a crush."

"The only things around here are soul sucking banshees and strays. Neither are my type."

"Whatever you say." I laughed, turning completely away from him prepared to walk back inside.

Before I could take two steps away, a chill ran up my spine. Alarm bells blared in my head as my eyes landed on a hooded figure standing in front of me. A cold sweat broke out over my body. The sound of a gun being cocked back and a deafening bang filled my ears, the wound in my side throbbed painfully. My stomach lurched.

My body shook, yet all I could feel was that deep, engulfing *burning.*

It's not Hawk.

A little voice somewhere deep in my subconscious whispered.

My breath stuck painfully in my throat.

They're too small to be that monster.

In the next second, a rough hand shoved me back, a body stepped in my place to face off with the intruder. It took me longer than it should've to recognize it was Singer.

"Well, if it isn't our favorite nomad in the flesh." Singer turned his head slightly so he could stare at me with an annoyed fire blazing in his eyes. "Alive and well after the attack. Exactly as I stated. More than once."

"I heard you the first time, screech." I grunted, pushing him slightly.

The shadowed woman's shoulders shook slightly before they raised their hands, knocking back the cloak. Dark forest green eyes stared back at me, an amused glint shining within them.

"What have I missed?" Dove's bemused tone brought a smile to my lips.

"Besides some psychopath getting the power to destroy the world? Clear skies."

II

"What are you doing here?" I asked as Dove fixed the cuffs of her sleeves. She grinned before turning her piercing gaze to Singer.

"I'll have to explain that in a more pleasant atmosphere." Singer stared at her blankly before groaning.

"I've had enough with you strays invading my home." He grumbled before moving past Dove and into the cottage. Dove giggled before we followed.

The minute we set foot inside; Lilly was in front of us. A smile the size of Rose-sea on her face as she eyed Dove up and down. After a while, she motioned us to the kitchen table.

"Please, come in and settle yourselves." She excused herself to the kitchen and returned moments later with a pot with a steaming liquid and four cups on a wooden tray.

She placed it in the middle of the table before pouring everyone some of the red tea. Singer plopped into a seat prompting Lilly to set his cup in front of him. However, when Dove moved to sit next to him, Lilly quickly blocked her pathway, the smile never leaving her face.

"Please, make yourself comfortable here." Lilly smoothly pulled out the chair two seats away from Singer, the smile on her face ever growing. With a small giggle, Dove obliged, grabbing a tea cup. "I see your mother has already planned on who she wants you with." I sputtered, shooting her a nasty glare.

How dare she encourage Lilly?

Dove took a sip to hide that mocking smirk on her face.

"I have no idea what you're talking about. The only person I'm promised to is myself." I huffed settling in the seat that Lilly already pulled out for me... right next to Singer.

"Of course you are."

I growled softly in Dove's direction before taking a sip of my tea.

A hint of strawberries?

"Besides, I'm not attracted to strays. They carry too many fleas for my liking." Singer grumbled covering his face by taking a drink when Lilly sent him an unsettling grin.

"Fleas? Why, our dear Jayde has none of those! Maybe you've been doing something to attract pests?"

"It was a metaphor, mother." Singer mumbled turning his body slightly away from Lilly as if he knew what he was about to say was going to piss her off. "Fleas, problems, death warrants - however you want to say it. If I want to adopt all of that from someone else, I'd rather that person be worth the effort." The next couple of seconds were a blur.

At first Singer was sitting in his seat- presumably giving himself a mental high five for coming up with such a good insult and the next he was sprawled on the floor with a rather large bump forming on the crown of his head. Meanwhile, Lilly was regal as ever, the smile on her face even brighter than before, but her teacup missing. I gawked at Singer's downed form as he groaned in agony,

Lilly's teacup lying innocently off to his side.

What's that thing made out of?

"Now, may I ask who you are?" Lilly stirred in a little bit of honey in her new teacup before bringing it to her lips, her eyes never leaving Dove.

"My name is Dove." She replied without missing a beat. I gave Singer one more side glance before turning my attention squarely to the conversation between the two women.

"It's a pleasure to meet you, my name is Lilly."

"It's a pleasure to make your acquaintance."

"What brings you here?"

"Of course. I'm here on an order from our queen."

"Queen?" Lilly set her cup down; her brow raised in a questioning gesture. Dove copied Lilly's smile as she took a sip of her tea.

"The fairy queen. She sent me here to watch over Jayde." Lilly's brow rose as her eyes glanced at me before settling back on Dove.

"Why now?" Dove shrugged leaning back into her chair.

"I wasn't told anything specific. My orders are to keep the last Henryk from harm."

"That's very generous of the queen, but Jayde is already being protected by Singer."

“And I don’t think I need to remind you of how well that turned out.” Lilly’s jaw tensed. I swallowed shifting in my seat as the temperature in the room dropped a few degrees.

Well, this is uncomfortable.

“Are you one of Bellatrix’s servants?” Only Dove looked at me.

“I’m sorry?” I cleared my throat, straightening.

“Why would Bellatrix enlist a regular human to serve her? I mean, doesn’t she need magical creatures to do her bidding?” Dove glanced away, a thoughtful expression on her face, her fingers lightly tapping on the table.

“You’re right. Our queen would never entrust a mere human with her orders.”

“Then why did she send you?” A sly grin stretched her cheeks.

“Simple- I’m not a human.” My eyes narrowed.

“You’re not?” A soft groan from my left brought my attention to Singer slowly crawling back into his chair rubbing the bump on his head tenderly.

“That was unnecessary on so many levels, mother.” He moaned. Lilly ignored him, taking a sip of her tea.

“To answer your question,” Dove began drawing my attention back to her, “I’m not a human. I’m a nymph.” “A nymph?”

“I knew it.” Singer scoffed, folding his arms over his chest.

Dove turned a questioning eye to Singer.

“Oh? How did you know?”

“I saw you fighting during the ambush. I thought it was strange that you could overpower most of the mercenaries even though you have the skill level of a toddler.” A faint blush appeared on Dove’s cheeks. She quickly raised her cup to hide.

“Very good observation.” Singer grunted.

“You make it sound like it was supposed to be difficult to figure out.” Dove didn’t reply as she took another sip of her tea.

“I’m still confused.” I piped in gaining Dove’s attention once more. “How come you don’t look like a nymph?” a defined eyebrow rose as she gave me a look.

“I don’t know what you mean.”

“Like,” I paused trying to think of a way to explain this without making a fool of myself.

Too late on that.

"Singer has weird colored eyes and pointed ears-"

"The only one with weird colored eyes around here is you, stray." Shooting Singer a nasty glare, I focused back on Dove.

"How come you don't have pointy ears or live in a lake or a tree?" Dove's expression was blank as if she was trying to process my words before a smile cracked her features.

"I see- you're wondering why I don't look like the nymphs in your fairytales?"

"Her ignorance knows no bounds."

"Shut up, Singer."

"Make me, stray." I rammed my elbow into his ribcage. His pained grunt brought a satisfied smirk to my lips. Before he could retaliate, Lilly cleared her throat giving Singer a warning gaze.

"Nymphs appear similar to humans." Dove continued completely ignoring our little spat. "To be honest, you probably have met some nymphs during your time in Redmage and in my village."

"If that's true, why didn't you tell me before?" Dove glanced to the side, opening her mouth to say something, but Singer's mocking grunt cut her off.

"Dove is a servant of the fairy queen meaning she can't just go around telling people who she is." Singer's taunting purple eyes turned to Dove. "Right?" Dove nodded in response.

"That's correct."

"Then why are you revealing yourself now?"

"My orders changed." She simply said pouring herself another cup of tea. "At first, I was told to simply watch over you. Then I was to keep you from any fatal harm, and now I am tasked with being your personal bodyguard along with."

"I'm not anyone's personal bodyguard."

"Oh?"

"A personal bodyguard is someone who gets paid in return for their servitude in one way or another. I don't get squat for dealing with this stray's personal problems."

"Then why do you watch over her?"

"Because my mother forced me-"

"Because he wants to." Lilly chirped, clasping her hands together. "The knight in shining armor always gets the princess at the end of the story!" She turned her starry eyed look to me. "Isn't that how your fairytales always end?" I nodded dumbfounded.

Haven't they always made fun of me for comparing this to a fairytale?

"Tell me when you see a princess." Singer muttered into his cup of tea. A soft chuckle left Dove's lips stopping my rampage against the insufferable fairy.

Now that I think about it, Dove looks a lot older than either Fawn, Cherry, or Apple. In fact, all three of them looked like small children no older than ten. Dove looks like an adult. Even the pixies looked childlike.

"Is something wrong, Jayde?" I blinked, focusing back on

Dove's intense gaze.

"Well, I thought Bellatrix only had kid helpers and, no offense, you don't exactly look *that* young." Dove tilted her head slightly, a contemplative expression covering her face. "Plus, why would you be using beginning level fighting styles? Aren't you, like, old enough to be more skilled?" Dove hummed slightly tapping her finger on the tabletop.

"To answer both of your questions, I wasn't born a nymph. I was born a human, but I turned into a nymph after awakening from a pixie." My eyes widened.

"How did you become a nymph? I thought pixies only turned into fairies?" I softly asked, my mind absorbing every bit of information that came from her lips. Surely if it happened to her then it can happen to Aric as well, right?

"That's not exactly true." She started clearing her throat. "If a child with the heart of a faye dies, they will turn into a pixie. It doesn't decide what happens after."

"What does?"

"It all depends on what you want to be." She simply answered. "Most people choose to be fairies, but others choose to be something different. There are even a few who choose to be ogres or hobbes. It just so happened that I wanted to be a nymph." I lowered my eyes processing the information.

"But..." I glanced away, digging my nails into my palms "how did you become a pixie?" Dove only smiled gently.

"It's normal to be curious." She dropped her gaze to her tea cup, swirling it lazily. "I drowned in a shipwreck with my family."

My eyes widened.

Way to put your foot in your mouth.

I swallowed hard.

"I'm sorry to hear about your loss." I whispered, looking up to face her. "With your family and the shipwreck." She waved it off.

"It happened nearly ten years ago. To be honest, I hardly even remember them, much less how we died." My hand gripped the bud in my pocket tightly.

"You can't remember anything?" my heart clenched.

Could Aric forget me too?

"Well..." a distant fog covered her eyes "I do, but only a few happy memories we shared together and a little of where I came from. I don't remember any details besides the basics of who they all were."

Relief washed over me.

So he could remember…

"What do you remember?" Her eyes rolled to the side, staring at nothing in particular.

"I remember that I was the youngest out of four girls. We lived in the country in Clearapal. My father was a wealthy farmer and my mother was an accomplished tailor. From what I can remember, we were on our way to Rosesea to escape a disease outbreak when our ship was overtaken by a wave." Her eyes narrowed in concentration. "I don't remember what exactly happened, but the last thing I remember is waking up in the forest surrounded by pixies."

"What about any of your sisters? Were any of them turned into pixies?" Her eyes softened as they moved back towards me.

"No."

So she was alone all of this time?

My hand unconsciously gripped the bud tighter.

"I'm sorry that you had to go through something like that." Dove smiled but didn't say anything. Silence encompassed us only leaving the sounds of the heated argument raging between mother and son.

I found myself not even focusing on the insults being thrown at my person by that insufferable fairy. Really, the only thing I could think about was what Dove told me and what that could mean for Aric.

That sounds selfish now that I think about it.

Maybe I'm obsessing too much about the 'what ifs' and the 'maybes' concerning Aric's future, but that doesn't mean I can be insensitive. Yes- Dove did say that it happened ten years ago and that she's accepted what happened, but that doesn't mean she isn't grieving. It's almost been a year since I lost everything, and it still feels like it all happened yesterday. I know people say time heals all wounds, but that's starting to feel more and more like a lie.

"Do you remember their names?" Dove's eyes lingered on me for a moment before they shifted to the side once more.

"I do."

"What were they?" A deep sigh left her lips.

"My mother's name was Adel and my father's name was

Braden. My eldest sister's name was Grace, then Cloe, and Hope." She paused, finally turning her head to look at me. "Why do you want to know?" A small sad smile trailed its way across my lips.

"Saying their names out loud without crying shows you if you've accepted what happened to them or not." A shocked look washed over her before her features softened.

"I'm sorry for your losses too, Jayde." A lump formed in my throat rendering any kind of speech impossible. A nod was the only response I could give her.

Time is crappy medicine.

"For the last time mother- no!" A low growl resonated from

Lilly as her hand shot out.

A pained groan left Singer's lips as Lilly gripped his ear pulling him closer to her. Pointing an accusing finger in his face, Lilly glared right into his eyes.

"You'll do it, or else." She warned. Confusion filled me as I watched the two.

What are they arguing about now?

"What's going on?" Lilly snapped her head in my direction; a pleasant smile plastered on her face and her eyes alight with happiness.

"Singer has just agreed to help you find supporters to fight Hawk." My eyes widened.

"What?"

"If Bellatrix has sent one of her own agents to guard you, then that means Hawk is finished or nearly finished massing his army." She paused, the smile falling from her face. "Which means he will be on his way soon."

My stomach dropped. My wound began to burn as I felt the air refusing to fill my lungs.

Hawk? Coming back here? Soon? It hasn't even been a month yet!

"H-How? It's only been four weeks- doesn't he need more time to gain followers?" Lilly's expression softened.

"It isn't hard to persuade people to his cause when he can control their minds." My throat dried. "Now you three need to do the same. I'm sure with all of the resources in Clearapal that Hawk has plenty of weaponry to beat you three easily. Therefore, you'll need to find people that will make this an even battle." She turned a bright smile to Singer. "And it just so happens that my son here knows quite a few faye who can help with that." She finally released his ear.

"Sounds like a good start." I replied. Singer rubbed his ear grumbling under his breath. I huffed, crossing my arms over my chest. "What's the matter with you now, Singer?" he merely grunted, refusing to look at me.

"Look, when Hawk comes, do you really think his ultimate goal is my death? I'm sure he wants something along the lines of, I don't know, world domination?" A contemplative look took over his features before he turned.

"Not like he can control me with that little rock." I glared at the back of his head.

"We don't know the extent of the jewel's power! If he kills me, then he could become more than capable of controlling anyone! " His back stiffened before an annoyed sigh left his lips. He whirled around to face us, his right eye twitching in annoyance.

"Fine, you annoying stray, but don't come crying to me when this doesn't turn out the way you think it will." A smirk appeared on my face.

"It's a promise."

III

"Look out for each other." Lilly told us as she waved us off from the front door. "If no one else has your backs at least you three should."

"Come back soon!" Claribel and Eallair called from her side, waving wildly with goofy grins on their faces. I couldn't help the bright smile that crawled onto my face as I returned the gesture.

"We will, don't worry!" I called.

"Be careful!" All three yelled back before Lilly slowly closed the door. I stared at the closed door; the smile slowly crept from my face as I thought back to what Lilly said when I woke up.

I wonder who I remind her of that makes her look so… regretful? Guilty? What could've happened-

"Get moving before you get left behind, stray." That is, until *he* spoke.
I can't have a moment to myself these days, can I?

"Why do you have to be so insufferable?" I groaned, following Singer and Dove into the thick array of trees.

"Why do you have to be an annoying stray?" He shot back without missing a beat. Dove giggled lightly. I glared at the back of his head before allowing a sigh to leave my lips.

No point in egging him on. Otherwise he'll never shut up.

"Where are we going anyway?"

"Don't tell me you don't recognize where we are, stray?" a low growl started in the back of my throat.

"Just tell me."

"Well, since you forget so easily, there are two things in this direction. One is that lovely inn we stayed on our first horrific day together and the other is the grand palace a friend of mine owns. Are you smart enough to guess who?" Ignoring his bait into an argument, I thought about it for a second before it dawned on me.

"Favian?"

"So you're not brain dead after all." I rolled my eyes.

Took all three brain cells he had left to come up with that.

"Why are we going there?"

"To admire the gloriousness of his estate." My left eye twitched.

"How about you pretend to be older than five and tell me." Even though I couldn't see it, I could practically sense the smile that spread across his face.

"Because he has the biggest following of faye that I know of."

"What about the armies the fairy monarchs have? At this point, they'll get involved given the circumstances." Dove said, a contemplative frown on her face. Singer scoffed, turning his nose at her.

"You're such an amateur."

I kicked a clump of dirt at his back. He only turned his head slightly in my direction with an annoyed frown on his face.

"Be nice to her. She's only trying to help."

"Then keep your bodyguard on a leash. Who knows what kind of mayhem she can get us in with her limited knowledge." With that, he turned completely around picking up his pace slightly. I glared at his back but didn't say anything.

I can always make him pay for that later.

"Is he always this grumpy?" Dove whispered in my ear leaning a little towards me. I smirked, leaning towards her.

"This is a good day for him."

"So he always acts like he's throwing a tantrum?"

"If you two have time to chat about my temperament then we aren't moving fast enough." We laughed as Singer picked up the pace.

What a baby.

***

When the sun began to inch towards the horizon, we made it to the place where we found Noel and Shadow last time. However, there was only one problem with that.

Why aren't we heading towards their grazing field?

"Hey, why aren't we going to go find Shadow and Noel?"

Singer glanced over his shoulder with a raised eyebrow.

"Why would we? I'm sure those two don't want to put up with another journey with you on their backs again." The nasty glare I sent his way only brought a smirk to his face. "They're on the other side of the forest this time of year. So, you're going to have to toughen up and walk." My face paled.

We barely made it to the inn before nightfall last time riding the horses!

"Can't you, like, teleport us there or something?" there was no mistaking the panic in my voice. I've seen the ogres and I've heard plenty of stories of them to know that they are not creatures I want to meet. Ever.

"What, don't you like to walk?" I grinded my teeth.

"Aren't you forgetting what comes out during the night?"

"What are you referring to? The moon?"

"No! I'm talking about large, monstrous ogres that eat people!" There was a short pause as Singer stopped walking.

"So, what's your point?" I let out a frustrated scream.

"We won't make it to the inn before nightfall by walking! Can't you get us there any faster?" A low chuckle left Singer as he folded his arms across his chest and turned completely towards me.

"You're so dramatic." Before I could yell at him, he continued. "If we make it to a safe place before nightfall then peachy, you get a cookie. If we don't, then I'll deal with the ogres while you cower behind a tree." I opened my mouth to argue but Dove slung an arm over my shoulders giving Singer a sly look.

"Don't worry Jayde. If the ogres come out just stick close to me. I'll make sure they don't eat you." Singer grunted, turning his back to us.

"You do realize the longer we stand here the less time we have to get to the inn, right?" My eyes widened as my heart pounded painfully in my chest. Without sparing them a glance, I took off in the direction of the inn.

"Hurry up!" I hollered over my shoulder as I continued to sprint.

Please- please let us make it there in time!

***

This is not good- not good what so ever!

The sun is already on the verge of disappearing under the horizon at any minute and we are still nowhere near the inn.

"What are we going to do?" I whispered, stumbling to a stop. My legs feel like jelly, my lungs feel like they're on fire, and my heart won't slow down. No matter what I tried, I couldn't calm myself.

How can I know what's coming for us?

"It's okay Jayde." Dove softly stated, moving to my side. Placing a comforting hand on my shoulder, she squeezed lightly.

"You're with me. Those ogres won't get the chance to eat you." "Meaning I'm going to be doing all the fighting as always when they get here." Singer grumbled, crossing his arms. He sent Dove a cocky smirk, "And since you've already witnessed how awesome I can be without doing much, prepare to be blown away." Dove merely waved him off. Singer mumbled something under his breath before making a face at the back of her head.

Feeling the need to protect his honor, Singer opened his mouth to argue back. The light quickly fading silenced him in an instant.

Oh no…

An angry roar echoed around us sending my heart into my throat. An eerie hush fell over the forest as if even the smallest creatures knew to hide. Heavy thumping that shook the ground grew closer and closer by the second.

They're coming.

"Come on!" Dove grabbed my hand and dragged me to the closest tree. It was thick, reaching at least ten feet high with branches covering every inch of it.

"Hurry and climb!" Dove wasted no time in jumping up to the lowest branch.

She reached down towards me, an urgent look in her eye. I swallowed before grabbing her hand. Using a strength I didn't think she had, she hoisted me up on the branch. Without waiting, she continued to climb as fast as she possibly could. I followed behind her, trying my best not to grab a weak branch and fall to my death. A few times luck wasn't on my side and I slipped from my place, but each time Singer caught me from below.

"Annoying stray." He grumbled before lifting me back up to grab another branch and keep climbing.

Halfway up the tree Singer stopped following, opting to watch the tree line in the direction the roar came from with expectant eyes. I kept climbing until I reached near the top where Dove was crouched on a steady branch. I crawled near to where she was but kept my arms around the bark of the tree in fear of falling.

My heart pounded in my ears as the tree vibrated from the thunderous steps. By now, I could see the distant trees parting as something big barreled through them. Another ear-piercing roar broke the silence. The fear felt strangling. My heart pounded in my ears. My shaking palms felt sticky with sweat. I couldn't tear my eyes away from the place I knew those monsters were coming from.

"Hey!" I jumped involuntarily before glaring down at Singer who merely smirked up at me.

"Don't scare me like that!" A low chuckle was his response.

"Didn't I say I'd handle it?"

"I don't feel reassured!" He chuckled again.

"One of these days you'll recognize the only thing better than me are the monarchs!" His gaze shifted to my side, a devious grin turning up the corner of his lips. "Can't say the same for you though." The moment the words left his lips, the tree directly across from him shattered, sending wood flying everywhere.

In the midst of the chaos, a hideous nine-foot beast barreled into the small clearing swinging a club wildly over its misshaped head. Warts dotted its face and wrinkles lined its two beady eyes in the center of its wide forehead. Its large belly shook with every step it took attesting to the many people it has probably eaten to gain such width. Opening its enormous mouth, rows of rotten teeth flashed yellow in the moonlight as it bellowed-

"Food!"

"Over here ugly!" Singer shouted obscenely, motioning the heinous creature over. My eyes widened as I stared down at him.

Before I could open my mouth, the ogre was already sprinting at our tree. My stomach lurched and my body shook violently with every step closer that thing took.

What is that idiot thinking!

When the ogre was halfway to the tree, I squeezed my eyes shut preparing for the collision, but the sound of a high laugh from Singer caused me to take a peek. In the next second, Singer leaped from his place on the tree and landed on its head. Gripping its tiny round ears, Singer threw all of his body weight to the left causing it to veer off course. Seconds before they collided with the tree next to ours, Singer back flipped off of the ogre landing in a crouch on his feet. The ogre, on the other hand, slammed headfirst into it, slumping to the ground in a heap motionless. Singer dusted off his hands before turning his gaze up to us.

"I don't see you proving my theory wrong, amateur. Why don't you get down here and take care of the next one?" Before Dove could answer, another ogre stampeded into the area swinging a crude wooden axe with a vengeful screech. Singer easily dodged causing the thing to stumble past him before it could catch its balance.

"You seem to have everything under control. Why do I need to intervene?" He only grunted in response, jumping out of the way of another swing from the beast. Just as he moved to dodge another hit, a third ogre lunged from the depths of the forest, batting him to the side easily with a tree trunk.

"Singer!" I screamed as his body disappeared within the brush. The ogres turned their heads up to us and howled.

"Food!" My eyes widened as I scrambled closer to the trunk of the tree.

"What do we do?" I shouted turning to Dove with pleading eyes.

Please tell me she has a plan?

"Don't panic." She started digging into one of the three pouches around her waist. "I have a plan." A few seconds later she pulls out two green vials.

"What are those supposed to do?"

"Stop them... hopefully." Without wasting any more time, she chucked them at the ogres.

The vials busted open on contact, engulfing their heads in green mist. They sputtered and coughed before their limbs stiffened. Deafening shrieks ripped through their throats before they went completely still. A look of relief fell over Dove's face as a triumphant smile turned up her lips.

"What is that stuff?"

"A paralysis potion I made during my alchemy training." I opened my mouth to thank her, but an angry grunt cut me off. We both turned just in time to see the ogres slowly flexing their bodies one by one. In seconds, they were charging at us once again.

I thought she handled them!

"It's not working!" I shouted, squashing myself to the trunk.

“Well, sometimes it doesn’t, but don’t panic!” She reached into another pouch and snatched out a small stick. I gave her an incredulous look as she stood up prepared to jump down.

What is she going to do with a twig? Poke them to death?

Bringing it to her lips, she whispered softly.

“Valkyrie.”

Immediately, it expanded into the battle lance I saw her use during Layne’s attack. Without sparing me a glance, she stood tall, watching silently as the ogres approached.

“I made a promise to my queen that I would keep you safe, and that’s what I’ll do.” My eyes widened slightly as she crouched.

Before she could leap down, a blinding light encompassed the area. The ogres shrieked in fear, covering their eyes as they scrambled away.

“The sun! The sun!” they screeched as they ran away just as quickly as they appeared.

The sun just went down, how can it be rising so quickly?

Before I could voice my question, it died down leaving only the moonlight and a smug Singer in its place. Relief filled me at seeing him alive but it was quickly replaced with rage.

Did he fake being hit?

“Nice to see I was right about the reliability of your skills.” Dove merely mumbled something under her breath, her lance transforming back into a stick.

“You’ve only seen my weakest skill set. If you had held off on that little light trick, then you would have seen what I can really do.” The smirk on his face grew as he crossed his arms over his chest.

“Be cocky after you’ve earned the privilege, amateur.” A frown marred her features.

This is going to go on forever if I don’t say something.

I sighed, turning a glare down at Singer.

“Will you stop pestering her? At least she doesn’t fake injuries just to prove a point!” Singer’s smirk never faltered as he shrugged.

So he did fake it!

“Since you two look so cozy up there, we’re going to spend the night here.”

“What about the ogres?” He gave me an exasperated look.

"Stray, what do we do at our homes at night that keeps the big bad ogres away?"

A barrier.

I glared at him, turning away to lean comfortably on the rough bark of the tree.

"Why didn't you do that in the first place?"

"Would there be a better opportunity to show your new bodyguard how much better I am?"

"You would think a *great* and *powerful* fairy like you wouldn't need all the theatrics."

"What can I say? I love putting on a show." I scoffed, closing my eyes as Singer set up the barrier around the tree.

The last thing I heard before sleep took hold me was the sound of Singer settling on a branch just below me and Dove settling above me.

IV

"It's all of your fault." Hawk smirked at me, the gun in his hand never wavering as he aimed it steadily at me. "All of your friends- they're all going to die and it will be all your fault." Tears swelled in my eyes as my hands clenched at my sides.

"Why are you always haunting my dreams? Can't you find something better to do?" I screamed back as the first of the tears fell.

My heart thumped in my ears and my stomach was a knotted mess.

Why can't I stop having these dreams? Why do they keep happening?

Why?

"I do have something better to do, but you're standing in the way." My heart stopped beating. "And it's my wish that you drop dead." The deafening bang. The unbearable pain. The endless darkness. The falling. Falling.

Wait... falling?

***

My eyes fluttered open only to see the ground fast approaching. A scream ripped through me as I threw my arms in front of my face.

This is all that monster's fault!

A pair of arms wrapped around my waist, pulling me quickly to a warm body. My stomach dropped as my savior flipped in the air before landing on their feet on the ground.

"I'm not going to be responsible if you die from suicide, you annoying stray." I glanced up only to be met by the agitated frown on Singer's face. I grunted squirming in his grip. He snickered, then dropped me. It was so sudden, I barely had enough time to process my butt hitting the ground.

"Ouch! That hurt, jerk!" He shrugged.

"You wouldn't stop moving."

I huffed moving to stand up, but a burning sensation in my stomach caused another groan of pain. I stayed in my seated position and lifted my shirt slightly to look at my wound.

It reopened a little l.

With an annoyed grunt, I moved to drop my shirt back when Singer grabbed my hand kneeling down next to me. I whirled on him to demand what he thought he was doing but only got a glare in return.

"Just stay still." I grumbled but did as he asked.

In the next second, his hand held a faint blue tint as he prodded my wound. Instantly, the pain was completely gone. Not even a tingly sensation was left.

"Thank you." I whispered amazed at his handy work.

He's almost as good as his mom is at healing!

"Do me a favor and-" he cut himself off as he looked me in the eye.

Are my eyes playing tricks on me or is his face getting a little pink?

His jaw tightened after a second before he whirled around with a forced cough. I narrowed my eyes at the back of his head before a sly smile crawled onto my lips.

I get it now.

"Don't tell me *the* almighty Singer is developing a crush on me?" He grunted roughly, picking up a rock.

"I've told you a hundred times that I don't like strays." He tossed the rock in his hand a few times before chucking it at a still sleeping Dove.

She woke up with a start turning a little too far. A short scream left her throat as she began to fall. Quickly, she regained her senses and twisted in the air, landing in a crouch on her feet. She blinked a few times scanning her surroundings carefully before her eyes fell on Singer. A glare formed on her features as she stood up, crossing her arms.

"What was that for?" Singer shrugged, mimicking her stance.

"I treat all of my charges the same. Get a *lot* stronger and you won't be in the same boat as the stray over here." Dove's glare intensified as she mumbled something unintelligible under her breath stretching her limbs. Straightening, her eyes turned to me as they softened slightly.

"Are you doing well this morning?"

"I'm fine." A sly smirk worked its way to my lips causing her to raise a suspicious eyebrow. "But Singer is becoming lovesick." The resounding hurling sounds from Singer accompanied by the light laughter between me and Dove filled the air around us.

"Let's get moving to Favian's place before you two make me barf."

"See? He can hardly stomach how much he loves me."

"What I can't stomach is your nonsense, stray." Dove and I laughed as we followed behind Singer towards Favian's home.

***

By the time the sun touched the horizon, we found ourselves in front of Favian's large estate. Its ethereal glow was only accentuated by the setting sun just as it was by the moonlight the last time we came. The stables made of rocks in the shape of twin wings stood tall and proud off to the side, an entrancing glow radiating from it.

"So this is your friend's home?" Dove absently asked analyzing the estate with appreciative eyes.

"What did you expect? I did say he had an estate."

"Yes, but I've learned to take what you say with a grain of salt." She smoothly retorted, crossing her arms under her chest. Singer grunted, a smirk forming on his face.

"A decent enough comeback. Can use a lot of work if you were trying to hurt my pride."

"I'm sure nothing I could possibly say could accomplish that." I giggled softly to myself as the two exchanged smirks as if signaling that a rivalry was beginning between them.

"Singer," Said man turned his head to me with a raised eyebrow.

"What do you want this time?"

"What are we going to give Favian in exchange for his help?" Singer gave me a contemplative look before turning to look at the estate.

"This is a rather large favor..." He tilted his head to the side in thought before turning to look back at me. "I'm sure he'll be perfectly happy if I give him one of your limbs." My jaw dropped as I stared at him incredulously. When he made no joking sign, my eyes widened.

"You can't be serious?" I screeched. He laughed lightly.

"If you knew how much a human leg or arm is worth to a harpy you'd think differently."

"No!"

"Come on- be reasonable! You'll be perfectly fine without one limb. You'll live!" I grinded my teeth as I glared hateful daggers at him.

"Then give him one of your-"

"Why do you keep teasing me by bringing such enticing prey to my home?" All eyes turned up to the balcony overlooking the front door to Favian standing in his usual black attire and a grin on his face. "If you're not giving them to me, then why bring them at all? You could've left them at that cozy tavern." Singer only smirked and replied, taking a few steps closer.

"Believe me, if they weren't under the vengeful protection of my mother, I'd help you season and roast them to perfection. Besides, it's too much effort going back for them." I glared at him, pinching his back. He jerked slightly but was unfazed otherwise.

"It's getting quite late." Favian called bringing our attention back up to him. He made a swooping motion, gesturing below him to the front door. "Please, come into my humble abode." With that, he turned his back to us and began walking out of our sight. "I'll be waiting for you in the study." Then he completely disappeared with the faint sound of rustling feathers.

"Interesting friend you have there." Dove mused walking past

Singer and towards the front door. Singer grunted walking after her.

"You're one to talk, amateur." He grumbled.

"So are you, psychopath." I mumbled following them.

We walked through the doors and headed straight towards the study. Instead of getting that creepy feeling that I was being watched the last time we came, the aura feels almost... inviting. The gothic style of the estate with the stained glass windows topped off by the occasional gargoyle statue wasn't as menacing as it should be this time around.

"Try not to have a mental breakdown in front of him this time, stray." I glared at Singer's back crossing my arms.

"That was a different situation."

"Oh really? "

"Weren't you there for that whole journey?" Singer grunted, stopping in front of the double doors to the study.

"It's not my fault you're a drama queen." Before I could respond, he pushed the doors open.

Favian sat at the head of the desk, his arms folded in his lap as he leaned back comfortably in his chair. A grin lay on his lips as he watched us with calculating eyes. He gestured for us to enter, motioning towards the three chairs-

When did he add another one?

- in front of his desk. Singer grunted moving to sit in the chair to the far right while Dove sat in the one to the far left leaving the middle seat to me. When we were all seated, Favian's grin widened. "So, what is it that I can do for you?" Singer scoffed, leaning his head against his closed fist propped up by the armrest of his chair.

"I don't need anything from you." He jabbed a thumb in my direction. "This is their mess to explain." Favian chuckled softly. Turning his feline eyes to me and Dove, an expectant look washing over his calm features.

"So, what favor is it that you need from me?" I glanced at Dove from the corner of my eye before sighing.

"Well," I started clearing my throat. "It's a bit of a long story." "It always is." He mused before relaxing further in his seat.

"Well, we need an army. To keep it brief, there's a sycophant that has a jewel that can control people and he's using it to start a war here." A brow raised on his perfect face.

"Oh? How is it that he came to possess such a precious thing?" I looked away, trying to figure out how to explain it. "Might it be the family heirloom you were being hunted for?" My eyes widened.

"How did you-"

"Because it's the only thing that makes sense." A bemused glint entered his eyes, a smirk raising the corner of his lips "Humans are simple only in their motivations. Since you were still alive, you were needed for either knowledge or leverage. Given you clearly didn't know anything, it could only be the latter." He tapped his finger on his desk, his head tilting to the side as we watched me.

"Although I didn't know exactly what it was, it was clear they were looking for something they could only get if you were alive. Since you mentioned a jewel... I'm assuming it's something one of your ancestors wished from one of the monarchs. In that case, he shouldn't be able to access its full power. At least, not without severe side effects."

No wonder Singer always comes to him for help first- he's better then the Guard!

"But," he paused, resting his head on his palm, "since you're still alive he wants to kill you so he can take over the world including the fairy monarchs. Does that sum it up?" I nodded, completely stunned. He smirked. "If you're looking for an army, then things must be getting close to falling apart. How many soldiers do you think he now has?"

"I've been doing reconnaissance missions for Bellatrix to find that out." Dove added sitting up straighter. "He has at least three battalions and a naval force." Singer whirled towards her in his seat, an angry fire burning in his eyes.

"Seriously? You never thought to say anything about that before? If I had known that then I wouldn't have come here first-" "Doesn't it count for something that she's sharing it with us now?" Favian placated in his eerily calm tone. Singer grunted, turning away and closing his eyes. He grumbled something unintelligible under his breath but remained silent, nonetheless. Favian's grin widened slightly at the sight of him before turning his gaze back towards Dove. "Now, what else were you able to find out?"

"He's using the jewel to force Lords and Kings in Clearapal to fund his campaign." Her eyes narrowed in thought, "However, like you said, I don't think he can use the jewel's full power. Most of the high-ranking nobility turned him away. The only ones that are working with him are desperate for power. They've been offering him soldiers, weapons, money- anything that he wants. If we're talking numbers, he has four thousand- a thousand for each battalion and a thousand for the naval forces." Favian let out a low hum moving his eyes to glance over the papers lined on his desk before giving me his full attention.

"You should know that this favor may very well be impossible for me to complete." My heart nearly stopped beating.

What? Then what else are we going to do?

"W-Why not?"

"We dark faye are not like the ones that you know." His tone was low and dangerous. "We don't fight for justice and honor nor do we fight to defend the weak. In fact, more often than not we are the ones attacking them." A lump formed in my throat. "None of my contacts will fight a losing war nor will they act until the fairy king orders them to."

"Well," Singer sighed standing from his seat. "It looks like you're screwed." Snapping my head in his direction, I glared daggers at his head.

"Shut up!" turning back to Favian, I gave him a hopeful look. "If you can't give us an army, then maybe you can tell us where the fairy king is?" Favian's eyes felt like they were piercing straight through me.

"The fairy king is not like the fairy queen. You'd have better luck trying to convince the ogres to fight for you than him."

"Why? Shouldn't he care just as much as the fairy queen?"

"Are you serious?" Singer scoffed, an exasperated look on his face as he glared down at me. "Were you seriously not paying attention the first time we came here and asked for information? I'm not going to bring you here again if you're just going to ignore the information given to you." Without looking, I stomped on Singer's foot. Besides a hitch in his breath, he didn't react.

Unhelpful jerk!

"The fairy king," My attention was brought back to the harpy in front of me, a bemused smirk on his face, "isn't one to care for mortal concerns. Neither monarch mettle in human affairs because it's not likely to involve either of them. Unlike the fairy queen, however, the fairy king is far more likely to make a bigger mess of the war, but considering he's in command of the fiercest army in the world, he doesn't very much concern himself with consequences."

"So you're telling me that not even Bellatrix will help us even if we asked?" He stared at me for a long while, his eye never once wavering from my own.

"Your war has nothing to do with either of them. They won't waste lives unnecessarily."

Then what are we supposed to do?

"Isn't there some way I can convince him to help?"

"He isn't going to decide to help you out of the kindness of his black heart."

"There has to be some way to convince him." Singer grunted folding his arms over his chest.

"If you really want to convince him, you should throw a hobgoblin at Hawk's army. Then he might be inclined to get involved since, you know, one of his servants was attacked." I whirled on him, a fire of vengeance fueling my rage.

"That is one way to sway the fairy monarchs to fight for you." Favian thoughtfully said, a small grin forming on his lips. Turning hopeful eyes on him, a spark of determination filled me.

"Are you serious?"

"Of course. Technically, if you were to throw a hobbe at Hawk's army and they attack it, then that would be a declaration of aggression to dark faye by a human army. Being the king of dark faye, the fairy king would have no choice but to defend his kind. So, yes, it would work." A large grin stretched across my face as I shot to my feet.

"Thank you!" Favian merely grunted in reply. Just as I turned to leave, my vision was blocked by Singer's frame. I shot him a look as I tried to go around him but he stepped back in my way. "What are you doing? Move!"

"And what stupid thing are you running off to do?" I huffed, crossing my arms.

"What Favian said. All we need to do is find a hobbe and make Hawk attack it. That way, the fairy king will have no choice but to help us fight him." To his credit, Singer didn't immediately insult me like he normally would. He just stared down at me with a blank steely gaze.

I don't get what the big deal is. It was your dumb idea in the first place- joking or not!

"There are so many things wrong with that plan that I'm finding it difficult that you just uttered such nonsense." My eyes hardened up at him.

"You were the one who suggested it- why do you have a problem with it now?" His eyes narrowed as he held up a finger.

"First of all, in order to send a hobbe to Hawk you would have to know where he is." Another finger shot up. "Secondly, once you do find out where he is, you would have to figure out a way to sneak inside his camp without any of the four thousand soldiers noticing you." A third finger joined the other two. "And finally, you would have to sneak out without the hobbe following you or any of those aforementioned four thousand soldiers finding you."

"Can't you do some magic to keep us hidden-"

"Even before then," his eyes narrowed further on me as he crossed his arms across his chest. "You would need to find a way to keep a three foot terror from being noticed all the way to the coast, then on a week-long voyage across the sea, and to wherever Hawk's camp is."

"Why? Won't it be easier to just-"

"Because if you wait until they get here then it'll be too late for even the fairy king to save the countless innocents that will die." His stony gaze never wavered as he leaned closer. "And people *will die*." A growl left my clenched teeth, frustrated tears burning my eyes.

"Again- this was *your* idea."

"An idea said with utmost *sarcasm*."

"Then what else can we do?!" The room grew silent. Singer and I were stuck in a glaring contest while Dove and Favian silently observed.

I don't understand. He's never acted this way before towards me- why is he being so pessimistic?

"As I said before," Favian chirped, relaxing into his seat, "it will be nearly impossible to gain the fairy king's support in this war. Perhaps you should try to recruit human supporters instead." My hands curled into a tight fist before a sigh broke through my lips.

I turned away from Singer, burying my face in my hands. Where can we get supporters? Who would want to fight in a war that is almost a guaranteed loss?

Everything is such a mess!

"If it will make you feel a little better," Dove pipped in, placing a comforting hand on my shoulder, "the nomads are willing and able to join us." I peaked from my hands to look her in the eye.

"How many nomads are there that can fight?"

"A little over a thousand and five hundred total in Rosesea." A sigh broke through my lips as I covered my face once more.

"That still won't be enough." The room grew silent once more before the sound of rustling feathers drew my attention towards Favian.

He stood from his seat, the wings on his back fluttering slightly as if he were stretching them. When they settled, his eyes glanced between the three of us before resting on Singer.

"You all seem weary. You're welcome to stay the night." He gestured towards the double doors behind us. On command, they silently creped open. I swallowed lightly before turning my eyes back towards him.

The last time we stayed the night Singer had to fight for his life.

"Are you going to be throwing another party this time?"

Favian's yellow eyes moved to me before a smirk formed on his lips.

"There is no need for that this time." He moved around his desk making his way towards the door. "Your scent is well masked- no doubt a result of your time with Singer and his family. I can assure you that no other hungry creatures will come to have a midnight snack." With that, he gestured for us to follow him over his shoulder as he crossed the threshold exiting the study.

We followed him out of the room and up the spiral staircase.

He showed Singer to his room first, then Dove, then lastly me. Unsurprisingly, he gave me the same room as last time with the same instructions not to leave the room in case some other lost soul comes to him in the night for information.

"Do you give information to everyone in the world?" A smirk played on his lips.

"Only to those that ask for my guidance and give me something in return for my services." He gently pushed me inside the room. With a whispered good night, he closed the door. I could hear the fading sound of flapping wings steadily growing further away.

A sigh left my lips as the exhaustion from all of the events that unfolded in the last couple of days took hold of me. I barely had time to slink over to the enormous bed before my body started to shut down on me.

What are we going to do? With just the nomads, we're bound to get massacred.

And why is Singer so different?

It's almost like he's... frustrated. Is it because of the situation? His own guilt with what happened with Hawk? Does he feel like he should've been able to stop it? Or is it something completely different?

Does he feel the same way I did when Aric died?

My chest tightened, the creeping exhaustion hitting me like a cannon ball. Before I could completely succumb to sleep, I dug into my pocket and pulled out the flower bud resting inside and brought it to my face. A faint glow emitted from it followed by the silent laughter of a little boy before it flared out.

Don't worry Aric. I'll find a way to end this mess so you can

live your life happily, just like you should.

Keeping a tight grip on the bud, I closed my eyes and drifted

off into a dreamless sleep.

V

Sun rays beat down heavily, causing a light sweat as we stood in front of Favian's estate. Singer was taking his sweet time exchanging pleasantries and goodbyes with Favian knowing that the heat was bothering both me and Dove.

Seriously, both of them are wearing dark clothing- how are they not burning up?

"Make sure not to get yourself killed on your adventures."

Singer grunted, waving Favian's words off.

"The day I get killed will be the day you become fairy king." A smirk cracked Favian's lips as he patted Singer's shoulder in farewell. Turning his eyes towards me and Dove, Favian nodded.

"I can tell you are still unsure of what to do, correct?" I swallowed, turning my gaze away from him.

"It's not like there's anything we can do at this point."

"In that case, you should head to Redmage." I snapped my head at him and blinked.

"Why?"

"It's one of the human villages that will help faye."

"At least the ones that won't eat them." Singer grunted, crossing his arms. Favian chuckled.

"They've granted me a few favors in the past, so maybe the stereotype is beginning to die out."

"Or maybe it's because you show some restraint and don't start eating people... or their pets." A thoughtful look crossed Favian's features before he laughed once more.

"I suppose."

Are these two serious?

"That sounds like our only option." I cut in giving the two of them a strange look. Favian just grinned while Singer paraded his usual smug look. "Looks like I'll be escorting you two around for a change."

"What makes you think that, stray?" I crossed my arms, a smirk forming.

"Because I've lived there."

"And what gives you the idea that either I or the amateur have never been there?" I grunted looking away from him.

"I didn't assume anything." I grumbled. Singer made a noise in the back of his throat.

"Even if that were true, I bet I'll still have to save the both of you for one reason or another." I growled and punched him hard in the arm. He didn't even flinch, letting out a hearty laugh at my expense.

"And with that," Favian began, a smile on his face, "I must bid you three goodbye." He turned around, his wings stretching to spread out on either side of his body before he paused. "One more thing," he glanced over his shoulder in my direction, a look that I can't place burning in the depths of his yellow eyes. "Don't do anything reckless that could get you all killed, little Henryk." A scoff broke through my lips.

"Why do you only tell me that?" I grumbled.

What have I done to make him think I'm that untrustworthy? He's friends with Singer!

"I only tell you," he began angling his body so he could look at me fully, "because Singer and Dove can both defend themselves if- and when- they do something idiotic. You're just a human. Do you think you can win a fight?" My jaw tightened.

Sadly, he's not wrong.

I glared to the side at nothing in particular, still feeling the intense gaze of the harpy watching my every move.

What does he want? For me to tell him he's right? Better luck getting Singer to say it then me.

Speaking of which, Singer snickered.

"Alright, that's enough mocking the stray." He started bringing my attention to him. A confused glare on my face. "Besides, I'm the only one allowed to do that." I swallowed, my eyes never leaving Favian's piercing yellow orbs.

In the two times I've met the creepy harpy, I've never seen him look so serious- or even hostile- towards anyone.

What's making him act like this?

A light went off in my head. Does he think that Singer will die? Though I'll never say it to his face, Singer is strong. He's always made it out of the toughest situations- no matter how much the odds are stacked against him. Plus, Favian has known him for much longer.

He should know better than me what Singer is capable of.

Or does he think I'm overestimating Singer's abilities?

My eyes widened, causing Favian to finally look away and focus on Singer. That look in his eye... his constant reminders not to do anything stupid- he's basically screaming in my face the consequences that will happen if Singer really does die.

If he dies, I'm coming after you.

I swallowed the lump in my throat as I watched Favian grunt at whatever it was Singer was telling him.

The two of them are close- maybe even like brothers. It makes sense that Favian wouldn't want anything to happen to his best friend because of someone else's mistakes. If he had any say, I'm sure Favian would've gotten rid of me during our first meeting.

If the situations were reversed, I would feel the same.

My hand slipped into my pocket and palmed the flower bud lying inside. I wouldn't want someone putting Aric's life in danger either. Even if he wanted to help them, I'd do everything I could to change his mind- especially if they were too weak to protect themselves.

Is that what Favian wants? For me to start protecting myself?

It makes sense. To them, I'm nothing more than a damsel in distress. I don't want to be seen that way, but what have I done to change that? If Singer wasn't around, would I be able to handle things on my own? Where would I even begin in getting stronger?

Who says I have to start with physical strength?

"Make sure to keep our rooms well dusted." Favian's eyes snapped to me, a question clear in those yellow depths.

"May I ask for what purpose?" A smile curled onto my lips.

"For when we come back. Plus, I want to prove a point the next time we meet." His eyes narrowed a fraction before they softened. Closing his eyes, he turned around.

"Then, I shall patiently wait for all of you to return. Good luck on your quest." And with that, he spread his wings and flew towards the back side of his estate. The smile on my face could only widen.

I'll prove you wrong. I promise.

"Well then," Singer started crossing his arms and fixing me with a mild glare. "You've successfully run off one of my closest friends with your foolishness. I hope you're proud of yourself."

Instead of arguing, I found myself laughing.

"Where are we headed this time?" I asked.

One of Singer's brows raised before he turned towards Dove. Even though I couldn't see her face, I could tell something was wrong by the way she tensed her shoulders. Her hands were stiff by her bags on her waist ready to pull out whatever weapon needed in case of an attack. Singer's brow raised slightly higher before he turned back to me.

"We're going to the inn."

"Will we make it there before sundown?"

"Maybe we will, maybe we won't." A sigh broke through my lips.

"What's the point in asking you anything?" He shot me a devious grin in response. With that, we headed into the vast forest with the sun illuminating our path.

***

"So what is the real difference between the fairy monarchs?" I asked Dove as we followed behind Singer. She raised a brow, turning her head slightly towards me. "I mean, I know that the fairy king is bad news while the fairy queen is, like, some kind of pillar of goodness, but what's the real difference?" She blinked a few times at me before turning her gaze forward.

"What do you want to know?" I hummed, contemplating.

"I guess... what are the differences in their personalities? I've met Bellatrix so I know a little bit about her, but I have no idea about the fairy king." I turned my gaze back to her in anticipation.

Understanding covered her features as she looked away in thought.

"In terms of their personalities, I would have to say that the fairy king is... sneaky. He never tells people who he is so people tend to make wishes without realizing it." She turned her gaze back to me, her expression unreadable. "The fairy queen differs from him in that regard the most." I swallowed, nodding before facing forward. I watched Singer as he skillfully moved across the forest floor.

"Have you ever met him? The fairy king I mean." There was a long pause before she sighed softly.

"I've met him twice." She began carefully. "He occasionally comes to talk to the queen about the state of the faye. I've even met his wife on one of his visits." My head snapped to her once more, my mouth wide open as I gaped at her.

"The fairy king is married?" She shot me a look, one of her eyebrows raised in question.

"Yes." Her eyes drifted off once more. "Though I was only able to meet her briefly. She and the queen absolutely hate each other."

"Why?"

"Because, your noisy stray," Singer nearly yelled, stopping in his tracks whirling towards us, annoyance written all over his face. "There can only be one fairy king and queen- hence why everyone refers to them as *the* king and *the* queen. The problem is that the king's wife likes to call herself the fairy queen." He crossed his arms, closing his eyes. "Obviously the queen doesn't particularly like that, so she calls the king's wife something else."

"What is it?" His eyes opened to rest on me, a smirk forming on his face.

"The faux queen." He turned around, beginning to walk in the direction of the inn once more. "Though I'm sure she calls her something else in private." I opened my mouth to say something, but the way Singer's entire body tensed as he stopped moving caused me to still.

In the next second, Singer spun to the left, his entire body crouched with his hands raised. Dove already had her lance out, holding it in a defensive position. All I could do was stare like a cornered animal behind them.

The leaves in the brush rustled slightly before a woman stepped out. I instantly knew she was a fairy mainly because of her pointed ears, glowing ice green eyes and dark, purple-colored locks reaching a little past her shoulders. The only other distinguishing characteristic about her was a scar that curved from the top of her forehead, over her left eye, and across her cheek. A sly smile sat onher lips as her piercing eyes watched the three of us with interest.

"Sorry to intrude," she mockingly said, the smile on her face widening into something almost sinister. "I couldn't help but overhear your conversation." My heart started to pound in my chest as I looked from Dove to Singer. Neither one of them looked as if they were going to say anything to the strange woman. Swallowing hard, I turned my gaze back to her.

"Who are you?" Her eyes rested on me, her smile softening.

"I go by Elah." Her eyes flicked to the side to look straight at Singer, her smile morphing into something dark. "Or the *faux queen* in polite company." Singer's eyes narrowed. Surprisingly, he still didn't say a word. Elah's smile widened as she turned her gaze back to me. "Though the title is only one reason why me and Bellatrix have such a..." she trailed off, her eyes rolling to the side as she thought of the correct word to categorize her relationship with the fairy queen.

"*Spiteful* relationship."

"What do you want?" Dove finally spat out, crouching lower in her battle stance ready to attack at a moment's notice. Elah didn't

look bothered as she lazily dragged her eyes to Dove's form.

"I didn't realize a servant of *that* woman would be in the company of the last Henryk. I wonder, why is she getting so involved with a human?" Elah's eyes moved back to rest on me, the soft smile returning to her face.

"What do you want? I won't ask again." Dove repeated, her eyes narrowing threateningly as she took a step forward. Elah didn't even spare her a glance, taking a small step towards me.

"I was just curious." The smile on her face lessened into something bordering on admiration. "What an... interesting thing you are."

"What does that mean?" I found myself saying without even thinking. My throat dried as her brow raised. I crossed my arms to hide my shaking hands. "You're creeping me out." The smile completely left her face for a moment before she straightened.

"Well," She started absently kicking a small rock to the side. "From all of the stories I've heard of your family it should be nearly impossible for such a precious artifact to be stolen. So, I was thinking: how pathetic does the last Henryk have to be to be robbed so easily? Maybe the family intelligence wasn't passed on to you?" My fear quickly evaporated into raging anger as my fist clenched into the material of my shirt.

"That coming from a *faux* queen?" her brow raised once more accompanied by an amused smirk. "You weren't there so you have no idea what happened!" A bellowing laugh left her lips.

"I admire your lack of fear," She started, "Especially when faced with someone that can easily kill you." My teeth clenched as I glared at her.

"But I know you won't." a curious expression covered her face.

"Oh? And what gives you that impression?"

"Because, if you do, then Hawk will have the full power of the artifact. Which means he could control anyone- even you." Another, more controlled laugh left her lips as she put a hand on her hip.

"You might not be as dumb as you look." The smirk made its appearance once more on her lips. "And here I thought the only reason you were still alive is because of your pet fairy. Without him, you would be reunited with the rest of your useless family." It took every fiber of self-control that I possessed to keep myself from

attacking her.

How dare she say something like that!

"You've had your fun. Now get out of here." I spat. Her smirk

just widened.

"You should watch what you say to a fairy monarch." I scoffed standing up straighter.

"Fairy monarch? Please! From what I hear, you're just an imposter leeching off of the fairy king." Something dark flashed across her eyes before a disgusted scowl covered her face.

"You filthy peasant!" She raised her hand, her palm facing outward.

A dark purple aura appeared around her hand growing like a flame. Both Dove and Singer jumped in front of me acting as my human shields, but something in my gut told me that their protection won't mean much against someone like Elah.

She may not be a real monarch, but she's still much stronger than I can ever be.

As the feeling of impending doom settled in my stomach, I watched as the purple fire surrounding Elah's hand morphed into a fire ball. She cocked her arm back, but before she could throw it at me, a larger hand shot out from the shadows of the brush and gripped her wrist tightly. Instantly, the flames were snuffed out. All the color drained from her face as she broke out in a cold sweat.

"What have I told you about messing with things that don't concern you, my dear?" A familiar baritone voice said from behind Elah.

She didn't dare move until the man stepped into the light. The minute I saw his eyes, I knew he was the stranger I met at the inn long ago. Those impossibly dark blue eyes with white lines running from the pupil to the outer rim.

What is he doing here?

"I wasn't messing with anything." Elah retorted, snatching her wrist from the man's grasp. She patted some imaginary dust from her shoulder before raising her eyes to give me a hate filled glare. "I was only disciplining peasants who didn't know their place." He raised a brow but didn't say anything. Instead, he fixed her with a misleading smile that she couldn't see.

"In any case, why don't you leave, hmm?" She scoffed, turning her body away from him and putting her hands on her hip.

"Leave? I'm a queen- I can do as I please-" Before I could even blink, the man had Elah's chin grasped tightly between his thumb and index finger, the smile on his face ever present.

I didn't even see him move!

"Why don't you head off and do something more worthy of your time?" The underlying threat made a cold chill run down my spine. Elah's eyes widened for a split second before she sneered, jerking her chin from his grasp.

"Fine." Her eyes snapped towards me, her eyes the embodiment of darkness. "Be grateful that I have a prior engagement to get to now." With that said, she spared the man one last look before disappearing in the brush. No one moved for a minute until the brush stilled. The man was the first one to break the silence as he gave us a teasing smile.

"Well, that seemed to have escalated quite quickly." He laughed before looking over the three of us. When he noticed that both Dove and Singer were still tense and ready for a fight, he raised his hands in mock surrender. "What's with the hostility? No one's trying to kill anyone anymore."

"Sorry if I don't feel inclined to trust someone like you." Dove snarled, lowering into a battle stance. The man looked thoughtfully at her for a moment.

"Someone like me? What's wrong with me?" Dove didn't answer, the tension in her body unwavering. Singer just watched, uncharacteristically not saying a word about the scene playing before him. Feeling the building pressure in the air, I swallowed.

"I've met you before." I blurted out drawing the man's attention to me. He barely raised a brow. "About two months ago, my friend and I," I gestured to Singer, "stayed at an inn. I remember a man- you- talking to me while he went to find a room." He cocked his head to the side for a second, a sly smirk on his lips.

"I remember that day. You seem... mellower now." I nodded slightly not really knowing what to say to that.

Well I'm not as clueless and desperate for answers.

"Yeah, well, who are you?"

"Who am I?" an amused tone filled his voice. "That's a rather broad statement, my dear."

"Then, how do you know Elah? Isn't she some kind of high ranking faye?"

I'd guess the only one who'd make her so afraid would be the fairy king, but what are the odds that he was just casually hanging out at an inn? Maybe this guy is just really strong.

"That's correct." His eyes shined with laughter.

"So, how do you know her? Are you close to the fairy king or something?" His eyes drifted to Dove for a split second before resting back on me.

"I know him very well actually." My eyes shined in hope.

"Then can you give him a message?"

"It depends on what it concerns."

"It's about-"

"The human amassing an army to attack the continent?" I blinked.

Has news about that really traveled so fast?

"Yeah." He made a small noise in the back of his throat.

"And you want the fairy king to help you with this problem in what way? Send his legions to fight the battle for you?"

"I don't want that! We just need *help*. Three people can't take on thousands of trained soldiers." I never saw him move, but in the next second that I blinked, he was standing only a foot in front of me.

Dove and Singer were both swatted to the side as if someone had kicked them.

"And what makes you think the fairy king will sacrifice even one of his people to save the lives of a Seelie fairy, a nymph and a human?" I opened my mouth to say something- to scream back at him that he had to if he didn't want Hawk to destroy everything we all know and love when it finally clicked in my head. The way he's acting. The fierce way he's fighting against my proposal.

The way he knows what the fairy king will think about what

I'm saying.

"You're the fairy king, aren't you?" A wide grin spread across

his face as he took a few steps away from me.

So, the fairy king was *just casually hanging out at an inn?*

Shouldn't he be too busy to do that?

"And like that the game of hide and seek has ended." He sent both Dove and Singer a taunting look. "Sorry for the shove I gave you two, but I couldn't have you giving away my identity to the girl so easily." Singer merely grunted dusting himself off.

"If I had known that was the reason then I would've told you not to waste the energy." The fairy king raised a brow to which Singer responded with a small snicker of his own. "I wouldn't have told the stray even if she begged me." I snarled at that heartless fairy. The fairy king laughed. Before turning his eyes to Dove.

"I hope I didn't damage your pride too much, young warrior."

"I'm a servant of the queen. Nothing you do can damage my pride." She firmly declared.

"As I thought." He hummed before turning his full attention back to me. "Before we continue, allow me to formally introduce myself." He made a sweeping bow. "I am Alastar," he stood up straighter, a mischievous grin on his face, "King of all unseelie faye."

"Why didn't you tell me you were the fairy king before?" I shouted. He looked away from me.

"From how you spoke, I thought you already knew." I raised a brow, confusion overriding my anger.

"What are you talking about?" He turned his eyes back to me, the white lines almost shimmering in his amusement. "You made a wish. Don't you remember?"

I did?

I stayed silent for a long while trying to think back to that day.

After a few seconds, my eyes widened.

You've got to be kidding me!

"That's why Bellatrix couldn't grant my wish..." I whispered to myself. Focusing back on Alastar, I glared at him. "Because I already made that wish to you." The king merely smiled, placing a hand on his hip.

"You really are a smart girl." I couldn't respond as my mind raced a mile a minute.

A lot of things that happened make so much sense now.

Layne attacking the nomads. Layne finding us at Bellatrix's castle. Hawk shooting Layne. Hawk shooting me- it all adds up. I made a wish to Alastar to know why my family was killed and I found out through a series of events that revealed everyone that was involved and their motives.

And to think all of this is because of some trinket my ancestor wished for.

"Did you know I was going to be shot once I found out the truth?" I finally asked.

He is the guy that twists people's wishes around into something that they didn't want to happen. Maybe he knew the outcome all along.

Alastar's grin merely widened.

"I knew something drastic was going to happen before the truth about your family's demise would be revealed. Exactly what would happen, however, was always a mystery."

So he didn't know.

I nodded absently, turning my gaze away from him. Before anyone could say anything else, Singer cleared his throat stepping forward.

"So, now we've established that the stray over here can't stop blabbering her problems to random strangers." The king let out a bellowing laugh before turning a grin on Singer.

"The stories seem to be true about you, young warrior." Singer grunted, crossing his arms and closing his eyes.

"Of course- what's not to brag about when it comes to me? But that's not the point." He let out a low, irritated breath before raising his eyes back to Alastar. "We need you to do what the stray over here asked."

"And, again, why should I?"

"Because he's a threat to you and your people."

"Is he?"

"Yes!" Dove pipped in, taking a step closer. Alastar merely shifted his eyes towards her. "Hawk could be on his way as we speak. When he gets here, what makes you think he's not going to try and take over your kingdom?" No one spoke for a long moment.

Everyone's eyes were on Alastar. He kept his gaze steady on Dove. After what felt like hours in the intense atmosphere, Alastar looked at me.

"Hawk hasn't proven himself to be an enemy of mine. He's *your* problem. This is a human war which means I can't- and won't- get involved." With that said, Alastar turned his back to us and began walking away. The path in front of him became lit with dark purple glowing pixies. "Until the next time we meet." Were his last words before he completely disappeared along with the pixies.

It didn't hurt to ask- even though we already knew the answer.

"Well," Singer began turning to both me and Dove. "Since the stray failed at negotiations, we might as well head to the inn. Might as well get some rest before choosing a suicide mission." I grunted.

"Shut up and walk."

VI

By the time the sun touched the horizon, we reached the inn. Much like last time, the dining area only held a few patrons scattered about at the tables. The barkeep stood at his post pouring some drinks for a few people sitting at the bar.

"I'll go find us a room. Stay here and don't draw attention to yourselves." Singer announced after Dove and I settled at a table. His eyes landed on me, a mocking glint forming in them. "Try to refrain from spilling your guts to strangers."

"As long as you don't do anything oafish."

"When have I ever?"

"Right now. You could've already bought our rooms, and yet, here you are." A snarky grin turned up the corner of his lips.

"I'd be a neglectful guardian if I left my charges without giving them proper directions."

"How about focusing on getting us some food." He made a face before turning his attention to Dove.

"Do you have money or do I have to provide that too?" Dove looked contemplative, tapping her fingers on the table.

"Isn't it a guardian's job to pay for things?"

"It's also a bodyguard's." He turned around and waved over his shoulder. "Don't forget mine!" With that, he walked up the stairs and disappeared. Dove spared me a glance before heading to the bar. As I sat alone, the weight of our situation began to crush me.

Alastar already said he won't help us until Hawk becomes an immediate threat to the dark faye. From what I learned from Favian, Bellatrix will say the same thing. So that only leaves the nomads on our side, but that won't nearly be enough to defeat Hawk if he really does have an army the size that Dove claims he does.

So, what can we do? At this rate, it's only a matter of time before Hawk takes over Rosesea. When he does, he'll be able to add more and more people to his army. Once he's done, he'll come after me. Who else will die before then?

"You shouldn't brood so much." My head snapped up to look into soft brown eyes. Dove gently smiled at me, setting down a mug filled with a sweet-smelling liquid and a bowl of steaming stew. "If you do that then you'll end up like that heartless fairy." I chuckled softly, taking a cautious sip from the mug before determining it was some kind of blended herbal tea. Setting it down, I rested my arms on the table and watched Dove for a moment as she began eating.

What does she think about all of this?

"What do you think?" She lowered her spoon from her lips leveling me with a confused look. "About everything that's going on, I mean." She hummed looking down at her bowl.

"I imagine my opinion is the same as yours."

"How would you know that?" Dove lifted her eyes to stare blankly at me for a moment before averting her gaze to scan the room.

"Whatever help we get from humans won't nearly be enough. In fact, it would only hurt us in the end considering Hawk can turn them against us." She turned her gaze back to me, a grave look in her eyes. "And even though the nomads can't be affected by the artifact while under the fairy queen's blessing, that doesn't mean they are invincible to blades and guns." I swallowed looking down.

"In other words, this is example 9,999 that we're screwed unless the monarchs help us." She hummed lightly, grabbing her mug.

"It doesn't change the fact that it is true. Our options are finding a way to get them to help, or we fight- and possibly die- on the battlefield." As she took a sip of her drink, she lowered it back to the table and gave me a sad smile. There was nothing more that I could add to the conversation that was already said a million times over. So, I just mirrored her expression.

"Geeze- who died?" I slowly turned to Singer's approaching figure, an exasperated look on my face. "You two look like your pets just croaked." A smirk stretched his lips as he crossed his arms under his chest. "Well, not like anyone is dumb enough to entrust an animal to either of you." Dove grumbled something under her breath, rising from her seat.

"I could say the same for you. Although you're more like a mangy dog being abandoned." The smirk on Singer's face only widened.

"I'll accept that for now." Dove snorted, crossing her arms. Singer turned his attention to me. "Now come on stray, our room is ready." I hummed, standing. Dove signaled to the bartender that we were leaving. We followed Singer up the stairs.

At the top, we veered off to the left. We walked past three doors until we finally stopped. Singer stood in front of the door for a second, fishing in his pocket until he finally pulled out a key. He unlocked the door before stepping aside. As I walked in, I noticed the room was similar to the one we stayed in before except this one held four beds instead of two along with three dressers, a wardrobe, and an extra door leading to a bathroom. A window was positioned in the wall across from the door showing the darkened sky outside.

"This one is a little bigger than the last one we stayed in."

Singer rolled his eyes, closing the door behind us.

"And here we go with the doltish comments and questions." He sighed, giving me a bored look. "Speaking of which, you didn't talk to any random strangers about your wishes did you?"

"Did you see anyone else with us? Or are you blind?" I hissed, shooting him a cold glare. A smirk formed on his face as he began to walk to the bed closest to the window on the right side of the room. "I'm just saying. The last time I left you alone it led to problems." With that, Singer dropped himself down on the bed letting out a long sigh. Covering his eyes with his arm, his breathing began to even out. Narrowing my eyes at his form I crossed my arms.

"You know, a real gentleman would wait for the ladies to pick their beds before claiming one for himself."

"Well, it's a good thing I've never been a gentleman a day in my life, ain't it?" He retorted without missing a beat. Rolling over so his back faced us, his breathing began to even once more.

"You're such a child."

"Sounds mighty hypocritical coming from someone like you." My eyes darkened as I thought of the many possible ways to stop his annoying yapping before a sigh broke through my lips.

"You're insufferable." I sighed, turning and walking to the other side of the room.

Picking the one closest bed to the window, I laid down letting out a deep breath closing my eyes. Counting to ten, I opened my eyes and looked at the ceiling. From my peripheral, I could see Dove sitting on the bed next to me, her back leaning against the headboard. For a long while, we all sat in a comfortable silence. Save for the distant sounds of ogres and the lit chatter of those still downstairs enjoying themselves- it was a cozy atmosphere.

"Jayde," slightly startled, I turned my head to the side to look at Dove.

"What is it?" She didn't look at me as she continued to stare across the room at the wall.

"What do you plan on doing once we get to Redmage?" I turned away from her and looked back at the ceiling.

"I don't know yet. It feels almost pointless going considering what we've already learned." silence.

"I have a few contacts in Redmage. When we get there I can have them spread the word to the other nomads to start mobilizing."

"Did you tell them the situation?"

"I don't have to. Survival in any war is never guaranteed. They all know what may happen when they come." She paused, turning her hard gaze to me. "They mainly fear what might happen if they don't- if Hawk gains *full* control of the jewel."

"Yeah, no pressure or anything." I mumbled letting out a sigh.

After a moment, a thought came to my mind and I turned my head to Dove. "Wait, downstairs you said that the nomads won't be affected by the jewel because of the fairy queen's blessing, right?" She nodded, raising a questioning brow. "Then can you, like, pass that blessing on to the humans we recruit?"

"Are you kidding me?" Singer groaned, shooting up. He rubbed his face irritably before glaring at me. Sitting up as well, I gave him a bored look.

"Are we being too loud for you, your royal highness?" He snarled.

"That, and your dumb questioning is giving me a headache." He sighed, bending his knee to rest his arm on top of it. "Someone like this amateur has nowhere near the amount of power needed to grant humans immunity to the jewel." I tilted my head to the side, a smirk playing on my lips.

"Well, you always say you're powerful- why can't you do it?"

He scoffed, tilting his head up.

"I *am* strong, but I'm not a monarch in case you haven't noticed. The jewel is a form of magic so powerful that only someone with equal power can counteract its effects which means only the fairy monarchs combined can do it. Anyone less would only make a fool of themselves. Now, if you were dead and Hawk was able to use the jewel's full power, then I doubt even the fairy monarchs together would be enough to counter it."

"Then what do you think we should do about this?" Singer's eyes narrowed before scoffing.

"You seriously haven't figured it out yet?" I raised a brow.

“Figured what out?” He groaned plopping back down flat on his back.

“What’s the best way to solve a problem?” I thought about it for a second.

“Carefully plan out a solution?” he growled, shooting back up into a sitting position.

“Idiot, the best way is to stop it before it becomes a problem- like how I should have kept walking when I first met you so I wouldn’t be in this predicament in the first place.” I shot him a dirty look before Dove’s voice cut in.

“So, what you’re implying is that the only way to defeat Hawk without wasting lives is to stop him before he comes to Rosesea.”

“Finally, I see some gears turning! They’re slow, but they’re still moving.” I blew a raspberry at him before turning to Dove.

“How do you expect us to do that?” Dove was quiet for a long time before a smile spread across her lips.

“A large army may be intimidating on land, but if you put them on a boat, it’s like shooting fish in a barrel.”

“Taking out one or two ships could take out half of their army.” I gasped, my eyes widening. This is perfect! We might not need the monarchs after all!

But there’s only one problem.

“How are we going to do that? We don’t have any ships nor can we fly.” Singer grunted resting his back against the headboard of his bed.

“The amateur over here claims she has nomads everywhere. At least one of them should have a ship, right?” Dove gave him an exasperated look before turning her gaze away.

“A few do have ships, but none of them are meant for war.”

Singer groaned loudly.

“What’s the point of having a ship if there aren’t any weapons on them?”

“They’re meant to be inconspicuous. How can they do that with canons?” As the two of them bickered back and forth, I couldn’t help but think over our dilemma.

We have a starting place, but how can we find a battle ship?

I thought back to the dock in Jancliff. We can probably steal a ship, but then again, won’t it take more than three people to man one the size we need? Commandeering is another option, but then we would be severely outnumbered and, more than likely, thrown overboard the moment we got into deep waters. So then, what can we do?

I wish Captain Jin was here. He knows all about this stuff-

My eyes shot wide open.

That's it!

"I know where we can get a ship!" I piped up, cutting off Singer's next tirade. He gave me a suspicious look before leaning back against the headboard once more.

"An idea coming from you sounds like a crime against nature."

"Do you want to be catty or do you want a solution?" I snapped back at him. To his credit, he at least stayed silent, but he did poke his tongue out at me. I waved off his childishness. "I know a captain that might be able to help us."

"Oh? What kind of captain could you possibly know?"

"He's an ex-pirate named Jin for your information."

"Alright, then tell us how an ex-pirate captain is going to help us? Does he even have a ship? Or can he walk properly? As a matter of fact, is he under the age of seventy?"

"For starters, he's actually mature- unlike you." I growled. Taking a deep breath, I refocused. "He has his own ship- with *tons* of cannons- and a large crew." Turning slightly towards Singer, I gave him a nasty glare. "And yes, he can walk just fine and is far under seventy." Singer made a mocking face. "I was thinking that, since he's an ex-pirate captain, then he should still have some pirate friends that can help us too." The room was quiet for a moment as everyone thought it over.

"If luck is on our side, then that might work." Dove chirped, holding her chin between her pointer and thumb in a contemplative way. Singer scoffed, bringing our attention to him.

"Even if I entertain that idea, how are you going to ask that ex-pirate captain of yours for help? For all you know, he could be halfway around the world right now on some island having a grand time away from mangy strays like you." I huffed turning away from him.

"Don't you think I thought of that?" I ran a hand down my face, taking a deep breath. "Look, before we leave in the morning I'll send him a message. It'll take us a couple of days to get to Jancliff anyway- not including the extra days we'll more than likely be in Redmage to try and recruit people. In other words, by the time we get to Jancliff, he'll be there." Singer was silent for a long time before he laid down with his back facing me.

"And how far away do you think Hawk will be by then? Better yet, he might even be crowning himself king of the world by the time your little pirate friend comes." I glared at his back.

"It doesn't matter, because even if Hawk does crown himself the king of the world, I'll just take it from him." It was silent once more before Singer snickered softly.

"Who knew the stray could be such a drama queen?" I blinked at him before coughing to hide the amused smile on my face.

He's sulking that I came up with a good solution to our problem before him.

"Alright, that's enough pointless chitchat. Stop flapping your gums and go to sleep. You two have to be a pain in my neck again tomorrow and I'd like to be well rested for the occasion."

VII

"How much longer?" I moaned, trudging behind Dove while Singer led the way. Dove turned her head slightly in my direction giving me a sympathetic look.

"It shouldn't be much longer. We're close to the border." I grunted, kicking a stray branch to the side in mild irritation.

"By the time we get to whatever village is closest my feet will be bloody mess."

"Fresh bread! Get your fresh bread here, folks!" Relief flooded me as I sped ahead of Dove and Singer. Peering through the dense tree line, the sight of a mildly crowded market square filled my sight.

"Finally- a town!" I clasped my hands together before whirling around to face my companions. Dove looked utterly amused by my response while Singer could care less.

"What are you so worked up for? We were heading here weren't we?" I rolled my eyes at him, placing my hands on my hips.

"Because, now that we're here, I'll more than likely be the only one able to get us around incognito."

"What ridiculous thought gave you that idea?" I shot Singer a glare.

"First of all, the last time I was in a village, the guard was very keen on taking Dove to jail so I'm pretty sure the bounty on her hasn't gone away just yet." A soft contemplative hum came from Dove.

"Now that you mention it, I have been seeing an increase of wanted posters of me around when I travel through the villages." She shrugged her shoulders letting out an amused chuckle. "Fair enough."

I nodded before turning to Singer.

"And do I even have to explain why it would be a horrible idea to allow you to communicate with anyone?"

"Speak for yourself, you annoying stray." I blew a raspberry, turning towards the village.

"Anyway, you two really should stay low. Plus, we don't even know what village we're in yet. I'm going to have to ask around." Singer scoffed before walking past me. He pulled the large hood attached to the back of his scarf over his head.

"You're ridiculous, stray."

"And you're a drag" Singer made a noise in the back of his throat.

"Whatever, but when you inevitably mess everything up, don't come crying to me." I mimicked him mockingly before following after him and into the village.

When we stepped into the market square, the shouts from the vendors raving about their wares filled the air. People weaved in and out between the stalls like they were dancing. Coins passed between hands for some while others were in the middle of intense barters.

Who should we approach first?

In the midst of the chaos, an isolated bread stall sat to the side of the path. An old man sat behind it. He was like a statue with his eyes half lidded, watching people pass his stall. It reminded me of Ginger's bread stand in Redmage.

Could he be a nomad?

Taking the lead, I walked over.

"Hello." The man rasped once he noticed me approaching. A little startled, I gave him a bright smile.

"Hello." The man nodded, his squinty eyes staring stonily at me making an uncomfortable feeling settle in the pits of my stomach. "Um, would you mind telling me what village this is?" The five seconds of silence that followed made the feeling grow. Taking a deep breath, I tried to hide my weariness with another smile. "You see, my companions and I just came from a long travel and we seemed to have misplaced our-"

"I don't see anyone else with you, young lady." I froze before quickly looking behind me. Sure enough, Singer and Dove were nowhere in sight.

"Right. Though, that's true," I started slowly turning back to face the man, "I promise that I am traveling with friends. They must have gotten lost in the crowd." The man was silent once more before a crooked grin spread across his face.

"Oh, you don't have anything to prove to me, dear girl." He laughed. "So, where are you traveling to?" I cocked a brow.

"Redmage."

He seems an awful lot like a certain undercover grandma I met a while back. Is he an incognito nomad?

“I see,” The man nodded his head, grabbing a small sack and filling it with two loaves of bread. “That’s a good city with kind people.” His mood seemed to drop as he tied off the end, a long sigh leaving his lips. “Though that may be true, you should be careful when you go.”

“Why?” I asked slightly on edge. Don’t tell me Hawk is already there!

“A few months back,” he began clearing his throat, “two of the new residents there disappeared. Some people say they were the missing members of that rich family in Clearapal that got killed nearly a few months back. Others think they were some sort of fugitives that were running from the guard.” He let out a puff of air. “But those are just rumors.” He held out the sack of bread to me, a smile on his face. “Who knows what the truth could be? They could be walking among us- good and well.”

Or right in front of you?

I restrained myself from bursting with laughter at the overwhelming irony of this whole conversation and took the sack from him with a grateful smile.

“True, but why are you giving me this? I don’t have anything to pay you back with.” The old man thought about it for a moment before he shrugged.

“Just take it as my thanks for letting an old man harp at you about some colorful rumors.” After a moment’s hesitation, I nodded.

“Thank you.” Tucking the sack under my belt, I looked back to the elder man with a sheepish smile on my face. “Now, could you possibly tell me what village this is?” The man blinked at me for a long moment before he slapped his forehead, a shocked look covering his face.

“Ah, that’s right! You did ask for that didn’t you?” a nervous laugh left his lips. “I guess my memory is going in my old age.” Letting out another laugh, he gave me another crooked grin. “This fine village here is Belhall.” I nodded once taking a step away from the man’s stall.

“Thank you sir, but I have to go find my friends now.” The man gave me a genuine smile before going back to watching the crowd with impassive eyes.

Definitely an undercover nomad.

I marveled before turning on my heels and gazing into the onslaught of people. They prowled the streets heading from one vendor to the next picking up the supplies that they needed.

Where is Dove and Singer?

Taking a few steps forward, I looked both ways hoping to catch a glimpse of my missing traveling partners only to come up empty handed.

"And they say I'm the one that causes problems." I muttered to myself, a harsh sigh leaving my lips.

"What's that supposed to mean, stray?" Twirling around, both Singer and Dove stood before me with three sacks- Singer holding two while Dove held one.

"Where did you two go? I told you not to wander off by yourselves!"

"Are you really that surprised that I didn't listen to *you*?" I opened my mouth to argue back when a thought hit me.

Can't argue with that.

Heaving a deep sigh, I eyed the sacks the two of them held.

"Anyway, where did you two get those?"

"Some shopkeepers gave them to us." Dove shrugged, tossing her one bag over to Singer. The testy fairy growled before dropping all three bags on the ground.

"How did you manage that with someone like Singer with you?" I asked, shooting Singer a teasing smirk. He rolled his eyes, crossing his arms.

"Unlike you, we know how to communicate with people. That's why we got free food for our travel and a ride to Redmage from one of the amateur's contacts." I hissed lightly punching the insufferable fairy in the arm.

"Whatever- don't run off again." He didn't even flinch as a smirk covered his lips.

"Whatever you wish, your royal pain." Taking one more swing at the horrid man, I turned to Dove. She smiled, turning around and walking down the road. Following behind her, I couldn't help but smile at the way Singer yelled at us.

"Hey- I ain't going to carry these by myself!"

***

We walked for a few minutes to the village's stables. When we got there, there were only a couple of horses and an oddly familiar looking carriage. My brow scrunched together as I surveyed it.

Where have I seen that before?

"You're here! I wasn't expecting you guys for a couple of hours."

I've heard that voice before!

Whirling around, my eyes narrowed at the sight of Dove and Cadian- the carriage driver that took my father and me to Redmage.

How does Dove know him?

"You should have known better." Cadian rubbed the back of his head giving her a kind smile.

"Well, I assumed that you would need time to get supplies for your journey, but knowing you, you'll manage somehow." Dove grunted, turning her head towards me and Singer.

"These are the two extras I told you about." Cadian first looked at Singer with a curious eye before turning his attention to me.

After a moment his eyes shined with recognition and he smiled.

"It's been a while, hasn't it, Lady Ella." He gave me a wink. I can feel my cheeks burn.

Did he know who I was the whole time?

"How do you know Dove?" I blurted out quickly. His smile only grew as he glanced back at Dove, a questioning look in his eyes. Dove only crossed her arms and looked away causing him to laugh softly.

"How about we get moving before I explain anything, alright?" I narrowed my eyes but nodded anyway. Cadian flashed me one more smile before turning to walk over to his carriage.

Opening the door, he motioned for us to get inside. Singer grumbled something under his breath tossing the three sacks inside before climbing in followed by a smirking Dove. Once they were in, Cadian looked at me expectantly.

"Aren't you going to get in?" I shook my head.

"I want to sit in the front."

"Why?"

"Because I want answers." He raised a fine brow before shrugging, closing the door. I climbed onto the driver's post; we all waited for Cadian to untie the horses and pulled himself up. Snapping the reins once, the horses lurched forward at a steady pace.

For about three minutes, we traveled in silence. Belhall grew smaller in our wake. Singer was surprisingly quiet inside of the carriage with Dove. After another minute, I cleared my throat and faced Cadian. He didn't even look at me as he kept his eyes on the road ahead.

"So," I started, gaining his attention, "how do you know Dove?" He hummed softly.

"Well, we're both nomads." I nodded, half expecting that.

"So, how did you become a nomad?" He was quiet for a long moment. As the silence stretched, I started to think I asked something I shouldn't have. I was about to apologize, but a short sigh left his lips as he tilted his head upwards to look at the sky.

"Similarly to you, I grew up in Clearapal. My father was a successful banker in the northern region and made quite a bit of money. However, my mother became ill after a rather brutal winter. My father spent all of the family fortune on her treatment, but... she died anyway." His eyes softened as he lowered his head to watch the road once more. A lump formed in my throat, as I looked away.

Why do I always have to open my big mouth?

"Is that why you moved here?" I whispered, afraid that saying anything louder than that would cause the repressed tears to fall. From the corner of my eye, I saw him nod.

"Our family was bankrupt and my father had to stop working to take care of me when my mother became bedridden. After we buried my mother, we had nothing left in Clearapal. So, my father packed our things and we moved to Rosesea. On the voyage, my father grew sick and died. One of the other passengers took pity on me and watched over me until we made it to Jancliff. When he learned that no one was waiting for me, he took me with him to the nomad camp.

"I grew up there. I learned how to survive and take care of those around me. Eventually, I decided to become a nomad and serve the fairy queen like the others. It was around ten years ago that I started this carriage business. With this, I can safely transport others like me from one place to another without getting notice." A silly grin stretched his lips. "And it also helps that I get a good reputation amongst the villages. Being the guy that brings supplies that are hard to come by makes you very popular, you know." My gaze softened. He kept his eyes on the road with a content smile on his face. There wasn't even a trace of sadness over his hardships on his face.

One day, I hope I can hold such happiness when looking back at my past.

Lowering my eyes, I folded my hands in my lap.

"I'm sorry... for making you tell me something so personal." A large hand patting the top of my head made me look over at him in surprise. The smile on his face only grew.

"I find that sharing stories- no matter how painful they may be- can spread wisdom in one form or another." He pulled back his hand holding the reins in his hands once more. "Besides, I've accepted my past a long time ago. Doing that gave me a chance to have such an amazing life." I couldn't help but smile back.

"Are you two done crying out there? I'm getting tired of hearing random people's sob stories that have nothing to do with me."

Whirling around, I opened the sliding door and shot daggers at Singer.

"Would it kill to have a heart?"

"My heart is a gaping black hole in which no love or light may escape." Dove, sitting across from him, giggled lightly. My glare darkened.

"Maybe that's why no one likes you."

"On the contrary, people love me, they hate you."

"Says the narcissist."

"It's called confidence, stray." I snarled at the mocking smirk on his face. A soft laugh from my left caused me to turn my attention to Cadian. I narrowed my eyes at the amused grin on his face.

"What are you laughing about?" He let out another chuckle before glancing at me.

"You two argue like a married couple." My face heated up as I glared at him.

"Gross!"

"I take offense to the insinuation!" Singer shouted, leaning his head out of the window. Cadian merely laughed.

***

About three more hours of traveling later, Singer was still whining about the long amount of time we had to spend in the carriage. Dove pipped in every now and again to try to make him shut up. Unfortunately, Singer is far too stubborn for anyone to make him stop talking.

"I'm telling you for the last time, you insufferable fairy, that taking this carriage is the fastest way to get to Redmage!" I growled at him. He scoffed, spreading his arms on the back of his seat.

"Please, I can *run* faster than this carriage."

"Then get out and do it!" I shouted back, my frustration getting the better of me.

I swear I'm going to punch that smirk right off his face!

"If I may interrupt." Cadian chirped, a hint of amusement in his voice. I turned back to Cadian.

"What is it?"

"We're here." Looking forward, the sight of Redmage on the horizon brought a smile to my face.

It's almost time to end this.

VIII

Cadian steered the carriage towards the little stables settled just outside of the village. We trotted along for a while until he suddenly pulled back on the reins, forcing the horses to a stop. My breath hitched as I quickly gripped the wooden seat to keep myself from catapulting forward. Looking at Cadian, my brow furrowed. I opened my mouth to say something, but his expressionless face told me to stay quiet. Slowly, I shifted my gaze to look at the town before us trying to see what could have spooked him enough to stop the carriage in the middle of the road. Almost immediately I noticed it.

Why are the Guard swarming Redmage?

It was like looking at a ghost town. None of the stalls or vendors that made Redmage a merchant hub were in the streets. Only groups of Guardsmen marched through the roads. Two of the three main paths leading into town were blocked off by a wooden gate reinforced with stakes. Only the main entrance was partially open. A single guard stood at attention. On either side of him were ballistae - heavily fortified arrows loaded in both. Even the stables were boarded up.

"What's going on?" I whispered, turning back to Cadian. He merely shook his head, placing a finger to his lips. I swallowed, nodding.

Pulling the reins to the right, he veered the carriage onto a narrow path in the dense woods to go past Redmage. From the distance and the long shadows cast by the descending sun, no one would've noticed us unless they were specifically watching the tree line. Given how the Guard were focused on herding the few villagers who meandered out of buildings off of the streets- we're the last thing on their mind. Once Redmage began disappearing behind us, Cadian's body visibly relaxed.

"Have they already been affected?" Cadian whispered to himself. I swallowed hard at the thought of all of those guards being under Hawk's control.

"They didn't look like they were from Clearaple. Can he brainwash people even if he isn't physically here?" Cadian only spared me a glance. He snapped the reins, causing the horses to lurch forward into a gallop.

"I don't know what the jewel is capable of, but I doubt he can do that." His knitted brow darkened his usual calm features. "It's more plausible that he has control over a higher up in the Guard and had them send an order to patrol the villages."

"What can he gain from that?" He looked at me from the corner of his eye. A chill ran up my spine at his stony stare.

"More than likely to find you." I gulped. Not being able to stand his gaze, I turned away.

"I get that's what he wants, but why the villages? Wouldn't it make more sense for him to think I'd be cowering in the forest filled with monsters?"

"True." Cadian started contemplatively. "Unless he was confident he could lure you out. If you had gotten away somehow, it would be a lot easier to catch you if you had nowhere to go." In other words, he's setting things up so he can toy with me later. My chest tightened, the wound in my side throbbing slightly as if taunting me.

"Aren't we there yet? My legs are going numb!" Ignoring Singer, I kept my attention focused on Cadian.

"When did the Guard take over Redmage? They weren't in Belhall." He glanced at me from the corner of his eye.

"I don't know and that's what worries me. I was just in Redmage four days ago and there wasn't a single Guard. Even *if* they aren't doing this to help Hawk, something doesn't feel right." I hummed, glancing off to the side.

That we can both agree on…

"Until I can get answers, I'm going to take you three to Jancliff."

"Or you can turn this little box around and I can do my own reconnaissance. I'll be done by the time one of you finds me something to eat." Whirling around, I slammed the sliding door between us open and glared at the irritating fairy.

"We aren't in the forest anymore, Singer. There are rules and regulations that you have to follow- and that's on top of staying incognito. If you make a wrong move, you'll get arrested. Then what will you do?"

"Break out and burn down the building." He shot back without hesitation. I glowered, but he just waved me off. "My point is that I'd rather deal with that than continue staying in this glorified cage. Unless you want to start carrying me around because my blood stopped circulating in my legs- get me out of this thing!" I huffed slamming the sliding door closed and cutting off the whirlwind of insults.

"How long will it be until we reach Jancliff?" Cadian didn't look at me as he snapped the reins making the horses run faster.

"It'll take at least a few hours, but we'll get there before night falls."

"Then make those horses move faster!" The muffled yell from Singer had a sigh leaving my lips, but I couldn't help but silently agree.

Who knew one of the few things we would agree on would be about travel time?

***

Just as Cadian said, two and a half hours passed by the time the carriage pulled into the port city of Jancliff. Just as I remembered, the town was crawling with merchants and sailors- royal navy men, pirates, and mercenaries alike. Though there were a few beggars lingering about and taking unattended merchandise, this is the best city in Rosesea to disappear. Even if we walked past fifty guardsmen, they would be too busy focusing on the hundreds of other crimes to pay attention to us.

Caidan stopped just before the stables at the entrance. He knocked twice on the divider before the door was practically kicked open. Singer ungratefully tumbled out, breathing heavily as if he was freed from being suffocated. Dove stepped out after. She was rubbing her temple, her eyes squeezed closed in annoyance.

I can only imagine what she went through with that fairy.

Cadian frowned at the dramatic fairy before hopping off his perch. I chuckled to myself as I climbed down with a little help from Cadian. He quickly moved to tend to the horses while I helped Dove grab put bags from inside. Singer plopped on the grass, watching us with unamused eyes.

"Who's going to carry all of that?" I smiled sweetly at him, holding one of the bags close to my chest.

"Our pack mule." Before he could respond, I threw the bag at his head.

He yelped in surprise, as the bag hit him square in the face.

My smile widened as I grabbed a bag from Dove and turned away.

Walking to the front of the carriage, I could hear Dove giggling over Singer's tirade.

"When will you come back?" I asked, looking up at Cadian as he climbed back up to the driver's post on the carriage. He grabbed the reins before looking at me with a soft smile on his lips.

"I should be back by tomorrow. If I don't have answers by then, I'll take you three to another village north of here." He relaxed back in his seat, the smile never leaving his face. "Don't worry, Jayde.

You have a lot more friends than you think." I grunted looking away.

"What makes you think I can't take care of myself?"

"I don't doubt it. How else would you have been able to survive for so long?" I couldn't help but smile back. He tipped his head to us as I stepped out of the way. Snapping the reins, the carriage jolted forward, heading back towards Redmage. I watched the carriage leave before a sigh left my lips.

If Jin appeared out of thin air now, things would be much better.

"So, what is your brilliant plan now? Go searching for your little pirate friend?" Singer taunted turning his back and walking away. I grunted walking after him with Dove beside me.

"He's an *ex*-pirate *captain*."

"Fine, then where is your *ex*-pirate captain?" I stuck my tongue out at him before lazily scanning the docks. I already knew that Jin wasn't here, but pretending to look would annoy Singer.

What he doesn't know won't kill him.

"Hm, don't see him anywhere."

"So, we came here for no reason." He deadpanned, stopping in his tracks in the middle of the road. His back was still to me so he didn't see the smirk on my face as I shrugged.

"We were supposed to come here after spending a few days in Redmage." Dove chirped absentmindedly as she glanced around at the shops. I nodded in agreement, the smirk on my face growing.

"If only we had some powerful fairy that could deafen you with his big mouth." Before the words could even fully leave my mouth, Singer was already turning on his heels, shooting me a menacing glare.

"There are many reasons why I dislike you."

"Touché."

"Jayde Henryk?" All three of us froze.

Snapping my head around, the sight of a middle aged man standing in the midst of a growing crowd of curious bystanders stared back at me. His clothes were tattered and covered in dirt. A patchy, scraggly beard barely covered his chapped lips. As he stared at me intensely, his dark blue eyes widened. He pointed a crooked finger in my direction, his slacked jaw showing off his rotting, brown teeth.

"It *is* Jayde Henryk!" he yelled at the top of his lungs.

My heart stopped as the crowd began to whisper about the last Henryk being found.

How do they know who I am?

My thoughts came to an abrupt halt at the feeling of someone grabbing my arm and yanking me towards them. As I regained my composure, I looked up to see another male stranger holding my arm tightly in his grasp, a determined look in his eyes.

"It's okay, Ms. Henryk. You'll be reunited with your uncle soon." He firmly told me before shooting a glare at both Dove and Signer who only stood in shocked silence. "Those two must have kidnapped her! That's why no one could find her!" *Kidnapped? Uncle? Who are they-*

My eyes widened.

Hawk!

The sound of the crowd chanting to catch the kidnappers almost didn't even process in my brain. What did he do? Who does he have control over to get strangers so riled up to find me alive? Why not convince them to kill me on sight?

Is he that desperate to kill me himself?

"However laughable it is to think I *willingly* took her, it ain't true." Singer deadpanned. A dark shadow cast over his features as he eyed the man holding me. "Regardless, I'm not handing her over to any of you." Before the man could even respond, a gush of air passed by my head as the man's grip on my shoulder simultaneously disappeared.

In a blink of an eye, Singer had my wrist in his grasp and was dragging me behind him as he sprinted through the streets. Dove led the way, knocking people who tried to stop our escape to the side. Glancing back, I could see the man that held me on the ground with a small crowd of people standing around him.

Did he really have to hit that guy so hard?

Just then, a group of seven guardsmen rushed out from the crowds and chased after us. A cold sweat washed over my body as I snapped forward and began to run faster.

"The Guard is behind us" I shouted as loud as I could to Singer.

"Oh, I'm so scared." He shot back. I growled about to yell at him that this was serious when he suddenly released my wrist. "Split up, now!" With that said, he turned on the balls of his feet and ran at the guards while Dove spared a quick glance backwards before veering off to the left.

"Singer-" My words got stuck in my throat.

He lunged into the air before using one of the guard's faces as a springboard to flip over the others and begin running back the way we came. A majority of the guardsmen ran after him while the one he jumped off of crumbled to his knees, holding his face in his hand.

Even after knowing him for so long, he never ceases to surprise me.

Just as I was about to turn and leave, another group of three guards came from an alleyway next to the fallen guard. They checked on their fallen member before their heads snapped in my direction. Without even thinking, I turned tail and bolted down the street, shoving people out of the way as I did.

I could hear the guard pursuing me- yelling at people to get out of their way. At some point, I heard a few of them yell that a hooded girl had knocked out one of the guards and ran down an alley.

That has to be Dove.

I thought as I turned a corner only to come to a halt. A line of five guards stood in front of me blocking the entire path.

"Jayde Henryk, I order you to halt." My breath caught in my throat as I turned to run only to come face to face with three more guards.

No!

My heart pounded in my chest as I looked between the twogroups of guards. One of them began to walk purposefully towards me before taking my arm roughly in his grasp. "We'll take you back to Clearapal."

No- I can't go there!

As the guard tugged at my arm, I let out a cry of pain falling to my knees. In his shock, the guard released me, opting to stare down at me in pure confusion. "What's wrong with you, girl?"

"M-my wound- you reopened my wound!" I cried without hesitation using my hands to cover my side where my gunshot wound lie. The guard's eyes narrowed as the rest of them came closer to see what was going on.

"What wound?"

"I was shot by a mad man. I barely escaped with my life!" *At least that part is true.*

The guard knelt down to my eye level and reached out a hand to move mine out of the way. Once he was close enough, I snatched his knife from his belt and hit him as hard as I could with the butt of it. In the three seconds the guards were stunned by their partner's downfall, I scrambled towards the crowd of people and ran. Quickly taking a hat from a stand, I pulled the lip as low as it would go and slower to a steady pace blending into the chaotic crowd around me.

Daring one quick glance behind me, I could see four of the guards rush out from the alley frantically scanning the area.

Good luck cornering me again.

I circled around the town until I made it back to the entrance. Pretending to look at a stall selling exotic jewels, I looked for any sign of Singer and Dove. It's a long shot, but wouldn't they come back here once they lost the guards chasing them? I mean, no one said where to meet, but wouldn't they come back here?

"Hey, ya'r goin to buy somethin' or wha?" The shopkeeper scowled, showing off his three missing teeth. I swallowed, shaking my head and walking away, silently praying that he wouldn't make a big deal of it.

"Hey, haven't I seen that girl before?"

Give me a break.

"Isn't that the Henryk girl?"

"Whoever she is- I saw her running from the guard!" I tried to bolt, but two men grabbed my arms and lifted me from the ground.

Squirming and kicking as hard as I could, I tried to escape.

"Let me go!" I shouted, flailing harder. The two men holding me were unfazed.

"We'll wait for the guard to tell us if that's a good idea."

This can't be happening!

"Let me go- please! You don't understand- if they take me back he's going to kill me!" Still, the two men didn't budge.

Blood rushed in my ears, my heart thumping painfully in my chest. My eyes burned from angry tears as I flailed harder. A frustrated cry ripped through my throat, but the men continued to ignore me. Flailing harder, I kicked as far as my legs could reach. My left foot finally collided with something as the man to my right collapsed to his knees. Clutching his groin, he let out a high-pitched moan. With my arm free, I swung as hard as I could at the other guy looking down at his friend in shock. Hitting him in the eye, he immediately let me go. Not wasting a moment, I scrambled to get away until a hand gripped my ankle, tripping me.

Leave me alone already!

"You're not going anywhere!" The guy groaned, still clutching his family jewels.

Using my other foot, I crushed his fingers. He let me go instantly. Shaking out of his shock, the other guy rushed forward as I finally got back to my feet. Just as quickly as he charged, he stopped. Before anyone could react, he crumbled to the ground like a sack of bricks. Standing behind him was Jin, repositioning his sheathed sword back onto his hip. He grinned pleasantly at me.

"Lady Henryk, it's a pleasure seeing ye alive and well after all of the rumors I've heard. What're ya doing back in Jancliff?" As I opened my mouth to respond, a loud yell cut me off.

"Halt!" We turned our heads in time to see two groups of guards heading straight for us. Panic consumed me as I whirled back to face Jin.

They can't take me back- they can't!

"You have to help me- please! I can't-"

"Later, lass! Now, we need to run!" With that, he turned and sprinted towards the docks. I dashed after him, the sounds of the guards pursuing us not far behind.

We weaved through the streets until we finally made it to the docks. A group of sailors that I vaguely remember from my voyage from Clearapal were lounging around in front of Jin's massive ship. The moment they noticed their captain running, they immediately jumped into action, pulling out their weapons.

"Capt'n, what's goin' on?" a sailor wielding an axe called as we ran past him and onto the ship. From the top of the ramp that connected the ship to the docks, Jin whirled around pulling out a pistol from his belt.

"There are guards chasing us. Hold them off until we get the ship ready for sail!" There was a resounding "aye, capt'n" before the men left to cut off the guards.

Meanwhile, the sailors on the ship jumped into motion, pulling ropes and raising sails. All the while, I kept my eyes glued to the

thralls of people who were now watching the spectacle.

Where are Dove and Singer?

"Now, what are ye doin' back here in Jancliff and why are the guard after ya?"

"I came looking for you." I turned to him in time to see the amused grin covering his face.

"If that be the case, then we will have to chat at sea." I raised a brow at him before I saw the sailors that went to hold off the guard running onto the ship. The last man stopped next to us, sweating and covered in blood splatter.

"We have a few minutes, but we must leave now, capt'n." Jin grinned, patting him on the shoulder.

"Good work, now make sure all hands are on deck." Turning to face all of his crew members, Jin stood up straight. "Set sail!"

"Wait!" I shouted, moving around to stand in front of him. Jin crossed his arms, giving me an even look.

"And why not, lass?"

"We can't leave without my friends. Please- we have to wait for them!" A frown formed on his lips.

As he opened his mouth, two shadows zoomed overhead. By the time Jin pulled the two pistols from his hip, two figures landed with a loud thud a few feet away from us. When they stood up, they turned. A sigh of relief escaped my lips as I recognized Singer and Dove.

"What- did you really think a few humans could take me?"

"They would have if I hadn't come back and saved you." Dove mused brushing a stray lock of hair behind her ear. Before any more words could be said, gunshots echoed around us. Whirling around, the sight of about twenty guards running onto the dock had my heart pounding again.

"Release all sails!" Jin hollered, running up to the helm while holstering his pistols.

The moment his hands touched the pegs, the sails fluttered loose propelling the ship forward faster than I've ever seen a ship move. By the time the guards made it to the end of the dock, we were already heading out to deep water. All the guards could do was watch as the sails caught more wind, propelling us further away. Jin's bellowing laugh echoed in our wake.

IX

"Now that we be in no immediate danger, why were they after ya?" Jin asked, settling into his oversized chair behind his desk.

I sat directly across from him. Dove stood in front of his bookshelf, perusing the contents. Singer leaned against the wall by the door, his head lowered and his eyes closed as if he were sleeping, but I knew he was wide awake.

"That's a long story." I swallowed as Jin gave me a look that screamed he had nothing but time.

What should I say? Would he believe me if I just told the truth? How realistic does it sound?

"I'm not sure if you'd believe me even if I told you everything. So much has happened that if I hadn't lived through it I would've questioned it too. The important thing is that a sycophant wants me dead and, if he succeeds, then a lot of bad things are going to happen." For what felt like hours, Jin stared unblinkingly at me.

Just as quickly, he let out a small chuckle relaxing back in his chair.

"Aye, I know that, lass."

"What?" Jin shot me an amused grin.

"I know what ye be runnin' from, but I see no reason to discuss it now ya don't have to give me the details now. Ye've been through enough today. Besides," he shifted his gaze between Dove and Singer. "I don't believe I've been introduced to ye're companions here." Dove paused, turning her attention to Jin.

"They're faye." I leaned back into my seat.

I'm pretty sure he knows about faye so it shouldn't be a problem telling him who they are, right?

He hummed in contemplation eyeing Dove first before pointing a knowing finger in her direction.

"Ye be a wood nymph, right?" Dove's eyes narrowed slightly as she nodded.

"Impressive you could figure that out just by looking at me."

"It helps when ye know what to look fer." Jin shrugged, shifting his gaze to Singer. "And ye are a fairy, aye?" Singer grunted, finally opening his eyes.

"Anyone with half a brain could figure that out."

"Especially with those ears." I whispered under my breath before laughing.

"Says the stray who thought fairies were fake." I waved dismissively.

"I didn't know faye existed back then." Singer growled at me before turning his head away from me.

"I guess your ignorance can be excused this once. Besides, you are a stray."

"Says the incorrigible fairy." A smirk spread his lips before Jin let out a short laugh.

"Ye two talk like ye've spent years locked up together!" he bellowed, holding his gut. My cheeks burned as I yelled at him that we *definitely* didn't have that type of relationship. Jin just laughed again. "Aye, aye, I understand." He chuckled, finally calming. "Now, what do ye be called?" He asked, looking directly at Dove.

"I'm Dove." Jin nodded once in her direction before turning to Singer. He grunted, sticking his nose up.

"Count yourself lucky that you've met the great Singer." Jin blinked before understanding seemed to dawn on him.

"Oh, ye mean your name is Singer! I thought ya was sayin' ye *are* a singer!" Jin howled. I can practically see Singer's skin prickling at the innocent misconception. I couldn't help but laugh along with Jin. "I be Jin, Capt'n of the esteemed Bird of Paradise."

"It's a pleasure to make your acquaintance." Dove nodded her head in acknowledgement while Singer narrowed his eyes accusingly at him. Sensing the hostility, Jin raised a brow at him.

"Is there somein' wrong?"

"I was just wondering how someone with a perfectly good ship and no physical disabilities came to become an *ex*-pirate captain." A spark of amusement entered Jin's eyes.

"Oh?"

"I've heard stories," all eyes shifted to Dove as she looked intently at Jin, "that there once was a man revered as the King of Pirates. His name was Captain Jin."

"What are you two talking about?" I interjected, crossing my arms. "Jin isn't some kind of-" A laugh escaped Jin's lips as he looked thoughtfully towards the ceiling.

"Aye, that be me." My jaw hit the floor.

"Look who's wrong again." Singer mocked. I shot him a glare over my shoulder before turning my attention back to Jin.

"When were you the King of Pirates? You only told me you changed because of a wish." he moved his gaze to me, a reminiscent smile on his face.

"Aye, that is true."

"Then, what happened?" he hummed, turning his head to gaze out of the little window at the waves outside.

"For ye to completely understand, I'd have to tell ye the whole story." Immediately, a loud groan emitted from Singer.

"No-no! I don't want to hear random people's sob stories anymore!" Whirling around in my chair, I put a finger to my lips and shushed him.

"Be a good boy and let him talk!" Singer glared back but didn't say anything else. Facing Jin, I gave him an apologetic look before motioning him to continue. He laughed softly before beginning.

"I was born at sea to a pair of bounty hunters on a ship almost as big as this one. Growin' up, I spent all of my time either playin' on deck with the crew or hidin' in my bunk while my parents fought whoever they were catchin' to turn into the guard. My parents were good at what they did. However, that brought powerful enemies on them.

"After turnin' in a high-profile mercenary, the rest of their mates found us and executed my parents on the deck of their own ship. Before they could do the same to me, a passing pirate ship showed up. They killed all who resisted and plundered their ship for all of its glory. The capt'n of the pirates was going to leave me be, but eventually took me in. Maybe she thought I'd be useful in the future.

Whatever the reason, I became a pirate at eleven.

"I sailed with them for seven years learnin' everything there was to know about how to be a pirate. In the seventh year, I led a raid on a fleet of mercenary ships takin' all they had and capturin' three of their ships. On that day, the capt'n named me first mate of one of the ships- with me own crew- in reward for me efforts. I was to command and maintain the ship how I pleased as long as I did what she said.

That lasted for nearly a year before war broke out.

"There was a capt'n named Blythe that commanded a legion of pirates that didn't like to abide by the pirate code. They attacked any and every one - takin' their territory. The capt'n won four of the five battles we fought, but by the last one, we were nearly out of crew, out of ships, and out of luck. In a final stand to let at least some of us survive, the capt'n held them back long enough for us to escape to Jancliff before fallin'.

"Once we reached the docks, the pirates weren't far behind. Almost everyone was slain. The guard got involved, but the pirates were merciless. With all odds against me, I had no choice but to run. I went through many towns and villages, but each one had more, and more pirates crawlin' around. Eventually, I was forced into the dreaded forest, but even there, they followed. I had to go deeper and deeper with each passin' day to stay ahead of them, but the further I went, the more dark creatures I found.

"It was durin' the second week that they caught up with me. I knew I wasn't going to best them in a fight. I was a man built and molded by the sea. I was barely alive by that point. I was delirious and starved, but I wasn't going to go down without takin' at least a few of those scalywags with me. I killed two of them before a winged beast appeared. It easily took out the rest with one dive. When we were alone, it stood before me, covered in their blood, watchin' me with bright yellow eyes.

"She watched me with hunger in her eyes, but she never came after me. Even when I ran, she continued to follow and do nothin' more than observe. It wasn't until later that I realized she was usin' me as bait since the pirates were still followin' me. Our relationship continued on like that for nearly two more weeks before she began to travel alongside me. It was then that I learned her name was Parsley. I guess it was originally out of curiosity that she began to get closer to me. But, as cliche as it sounds, we fell in love after some time.

"We built a house together near the heart of the forest. We lived there for nearly a year before the pirates found me once more. Apparently, a war began between the pirates because of Capt'n Blythe's attacks. Pirates tryin' to escape the carnage fled into the forest followed by Blythe's men. Most of them were killed by the dark faye, but there were far too many for them all to be wiped out. Nearly thirty pirates came to our home. We tried our best to fight them off, but in the end, it was a fruitless effort. I was knocked down when six of them surrounded me. Parsley tried to save me, but in the end, one of the bastards cut off half of her left wing. Beaten, and far too injured, I could only watch as they prepared to kill my beloved before my eyes, but before they could, a man appeared in a flash of white takin' out the lot of them with only a flick of his wrist.

"When they were dead, he went straight to Parsley, checkin' on her wing and her other injuries. At the time, I didn't know who he was, so I was goin' to fight him when he asked me what I was doin' this far into the forest. I wanted to tell'em to stick to his own business, but he'd just saved us. It goes against the code to show hostility to someone that saved ya. So, I told'em the truth. He then told me he was the King of Dark Faye. He said that, if I wished it, then he could heal Parsley. By then, she had lost so much blood..." his voice trailed off, a far away look in his eyes. He rubbed his eyes, a deep sigh leaving his lips. "I told him that my wish was to heal her. I never thought doin' so would cost me everythin'.

"Alast, he waved his hand and she turned into this... light. A little, dark purple thing. At the time, I had no idea what happen'd. Bein' a young and dumb lad, I tried to fight him- but I learned quickly king wasn't a title he was just givin'." He shook his head, scratching the side of his cheek. "Anyway, that's when he told me the price that came with my wish- the price that *had* to be paid. That bein' I would never see her again.

"To say I was devastated wouldn't do what I felt that day justice. Parsley was too wounded for any amount of magic to save her current body. The only way to save her was for him to turn her into a pixie. That way, she would either emerge with a new body or..." his jaw tightened, his eyes holding a faraway look in them. Clearing his throat, he continued quietly. "Well... I think you get the picture."

"I asked him how long it would take for her to turn back into Parsley... but he said it's impossible to know. Apparently, some transform in a few hours while others take days, months, years, decades, and even centuries. It was that moment that I truly understood what he meant about the *price*." I swallowed, Aric's bud felt like it weighed a thousand pounds in my pocket.

"Did you... ever see her again? I know you said what the price was but... I mean- did you ever see her in passing at least?"

Is it selfish that I'm thinking of my brother in this situation?

Clearly Jin is still affected by this, but I can't help it. What if... what if by hearing this tale, it'll give me hints about my own future?

The corner of his lips turned up halfheartedly, as he shook his head minutely. A lump formed in my throat. Balling the fabric of my skirt, I turned away.

So, there may be a chance I'll never see Aric again...

"Then, what did you do?" He shrugged, slumping back into his chair.

"I made a vow." He simply said. "Since I didn't have the power to protect the one I loved, then I would become strong enough to make the world safer." His jaw tensed before he let out a deep breath. "After all that, I had nowhere to go- no one left in the world to turn to. So, I headed back to Jancliff knowin' full well that the pirate war was still being waged on the seas, but there was nothin' else I could think of doing. The forest only reminded me what I'd lost and I couldn't spend the rest of my days hidin' from my past.

"Nearly four weeks later I made it to Redmage- half delirious from grief and sleep deprivation. The state of the village then showed just how *ugly* the war had gotten. The hospital overrun with bodies, children left orphaned flooded the alleys, and widows haunted the streets like lost apparitions. It just reminded me how *pointless* it all was. Then again, that's how wars like that are. Only fueled by the greed of a few but paid in the blood of the many." He shook his head, a dark glint entering his eyes.

"I found other pirates who fled the war in the inn. Must've been fate as they held the same thoughts as I did. We recruited enough to make a small crew then headed to Jancliff. There, we gained more crew mates while we waitin' for a good enough ship to snatch.

"To make a long story short, we sailed for two days, takin' down small fleets who sailed under the flag of Capt'n Blythe. Eventually, we got his attention. He came at us with all he had- a fleet of nearly twenty-five ships- while we were only four strong. From the outside, it would seem like he had us beat, but those who think so have never met me!" He grinned, the dark cloud that was covering him finally dissipating.

"The battle lasted nearly two days, but eventually we were able to damage Capt'n Blythe's lead ship enough to board it. While my men took out his crew, I took out Blythe. After one of the most gruesome battles I've ever fought, we came out victorious. We had ended the dreaded pirate wars that waged upon the seas for nearly two years in four days. Once the news spread of our victory, nearly all survivin' pirate capt'ns and rogue pirates joined us. After we gained a following of over a hundred ships, I was named the King of Pirates.

"I held onto the title for six years, though I never called myself that. I only used the power it granted to fulfill my oath to make the world a little safer for my love when she came back. I kept the peace on the seas and stopped corruption when it sprouted its ugly head in both the naval forces and in my own order. I sailed under the flag that held my love's favorite flower, until the day I met the fairy king once more.

"He appeared out of thin air on the deck of my ship. He was almost like a statue- just lookin' across the open waters like he was contemplatin' somethin'. I don't know what business a faye monarch would have with me unless it had to do with Parsley. So, I asked if she had come back- if she had finally awakened. Instead, he told me that she was dying." His jaw clenched, his back straightened as his eyes burned with a fiery rage. "How could that happen? He took her- changed her into a pixie to *save* her. How could she be dyin' now?" He ran a frustrated hand down his face.

"'I can't control fate' he says. Then what was the point of takin' her from me?" He huffed, pausing for a moment to rein in his rage. After a few seconds, he continued. "I ain't ashamed to say I begged- pleaded with him. At first, he said I'd already used my wish, but why else would he have come if he truly couldn't do anythin'?

Eventually, we made a deal. He would save her if I gave up the title as King of Pirates." His brow knitted slightly. "I still don't know why that was the price, but if it meant she would live, it's meaningless.

"Before he left, he warned me that Parsley might not remember me when she transforms. I felt... hesitant, but I refused to change my mind. If she didn't recognize me, it would break my heart, but I'd rather that than livin' on regrettin' I let her die knowin' I could've done somethin'. After that, he left.

"It's been six years. The Pirate King's flag hasn't been flown from any helm since that day. Though there are still those who still call me that, I refuse to use it. Besides, when I do visit Rosesea, I can *feel* her presence- and that's enough for me." As his tale came to its end, the room was bathed in silence. No one wanted to be the first to speak after an ending like that. Is that why he told me to be careful with my wishes?

Look how well you followed that advice.

I silently scolded myself for my ignorance. Even back then, I should've taken his advice to heart. He's always looked out for me - I should've known. He told me that for a reason.

Especially since he could've ignored me and just taken the money.

A soft chuckle brought my attention back to Jin, a small grin settled on his lips.

"What's with those faces? Don't be gettin' down on my account!" I couldn't help but give him a sad smile in return.

How can he still be so boisterous?

"Please," Singer scoffed, crossing his arms and holding his head up a little higher. "I was just thinking you quit the dream life too easily. What if the king was playing you? You just gave it up - no questions asked- *and* it was over a girl."

"Singer!" I snapped in his direction shooting him a glare. Honestly, does he even know the meaning of the word compassion? A louder laugh left Jin's lips as he leveled Singer with a knowing grin, waving off my apologies.

"One day, you'll know what it's like to want to sacrifice yourself for someone you love. Maybe sooner than you think." Singer grimaced, turning his nose up.

"How much do you wanna bet?"

"I'd stake my-" a deafening bang drowned out Jin's voice. The ship shook violently, knocking everyone off balance.

"What was that?" Jin didn't even spare me a glance as he bolted from the room. Singer, Dove, and I were close behind him. The moment we stepped foot on deck, a cloud of sorrow befell us.

Stationed in front of us were four large naval ships flying a flag that chilled my bones. The air in my lungs thickened as my eyes widened in horror.

Hawk!

There was no mistaking it. The flag that flew above all four ships was a dead giveaway. Even if you didn't know all of the country flags in Clearapal, it would still be a dead giveaway. Besides, what country would make their flag a moonstone covered in blood?

X

"Ready the canons!" Jin shouted over the roar of the sea and the volley of artillery fire from Hawk's ships.

"Aye, capt'n!" He didn't waste another second as he took long strides up the short staircase to the helm. Taking it into his hands he turned it sharply, quickly turning the ship to the side just as another barrage was fired.

How did he get here so quickly?

"If you're too scared to help then get below deck, stray!" Singer scoffed at me before running towards a group of sailors struggling to load a cannon as the ship rocked violently. What does he expect me to do anyway? Magically get rid of the enemy with a wave of my hand?

He should be the one doing that!

"It's alright, Jayde." Dove's comforting hand clasping my shoulder calmed me slightly. Glancing up at her, she gave me a reassuring grin. "Stay calm and do what you can. Just remember- no matter what happens- you *have* to stay alive." With that, she sprinted off towards a group of sailors passing out rifles.

Grabbing one, she raced alongside the sailors to the side of the ship. Lining up in three rows of five, they fired volley after volley at the enemy. Most of them hit their mark, but it was like there was an endless supply of them. As one fell, another took their place. Taking in a deep breath, I made a move to head back inside when a thought occurred to me.

I may not be skilled enough to fight, but I can still help Jin!

Not giving myself time to rationalize why it was a bad idea, I twirled on the balls of my feet and ran up the steps to the helm. Jin held the helm in his hands, his hard eyes assessing the situation with seasoned confidence.

"Jin," he turned his head completely towards me, a good-natured grin forming on his face. I swallowed before steeling myself. "I want to help." He watched me for a second longer before throwing his head back in amusement.

"Even with cannon fire threatenin' to send us to the netherworld ye still stand here with the same spirit as ye do when addressing the fairy sprite!" He motioned for me to come closer before gesturing to the safety railing in front of the helm. "Ye can be my temporary first mate. Relay my orders to the crew and tell me what I can't see. Ye have to be quick about it- ye are my eyes and ears." I nodded before scanning the situation.

To say everything was in chaos would be the understatement of the century.

The first wave of cannon fire did serious damage to the right side of the ship. Two of the cannons were basically useless while a chunk was blown off our front. Even though we have well over thirty cannons, the look on Jin's face suggested losing any of them is dire. Jin's eyes suddenly darted towards the enemy ships before he swiftly spun the wheel to the right.

"Tell the lads to raise the sails!" he shouted, not a single hint of playfulness left in his voice. Nodding absently, I turned back towards the deck taking a second to clear my throat.

"Raise the sails!" I screamed as loud as I could.

Some of the men looked taken aback and glanced in my direction for a moment before quickly scrambling to do as I said with a resounding "aye". Seconds later, the sails of the ship raised in record time allowing Jin to turn the ship much faster. Moments later, a barrage of artillery hit the water where we once were.

"Load the cannons and fire on my command!" Jin shouted to me as he began turning us around.

"Load the cannons!" I repeated with the same response from the crew. They moved with practiced grace- the cannons were loaded and aligned in record time. The crew stood ready, waiting for the order to fire at on a hairs notice.

How many of them fought in the wars with Jin?

"Steady now!" Jin shouted as the ship made a sharp turn angling the sides of the ship so that the cannons were perfectly aimed at the four ships. "Fire!"

With a thunderous boom, the crew fired their deadly projectiles.

The artillery whizzed through the air before striking their targets. A shrill groan echoed before the large supporting beam in the middle of the first ship gave way crashing into the deck. The screams from the sailors were drowned out as the wood split and cracked. With a final bang from its belly, the ship exploded. Chunks of debris and bodies shot into the air before slamming back into the ocean.

Whatever was left of the ship sunk with violent bubbles.

Not long after, two of the other ships became covered in smoke. Crew members were bailing into the thrashing waters in droves. Just as both vessels began to groan, they also detonated. Those who didn't make it off plummeted to the icy depths along with the remains.

The last boat must've decided to cut their losses. Without so much as retaliating, they turned tail and ran.

"We did it!" one of the crew members shouted before the deck was engulfed in an uproar of cheers. I couldn't help but smile.

Maybe we do have a chance of beating Hawk. At least, with Jin's help.

"Silence your howlin'!" Jin yelled over the celebration.

A hush immediately swept over the crew as they looked towards their captain, but he was focused on something in the distance. Following his gaze, my heart immediately fell into my stomach as my throat dried.

Why can't he just let me have one moment of peace?

On the horizon were twelve ships. Each was equipped with nearly fifty cannons. Even from my vantage point, I could see nearly a hundred sailors prepping for battle in fluid sequences. Hawk's flag flew above them, flapping in the wind like a proud novelty of the future.

Why can't he ever fight fair?!

I could practically feel the cloud of dread fall over Jin's men.

"Am I smellin' fear from my crew?" Jin suddenly hollered. I gave him a shocked look, opening my mouth to say something, but Jin raised a silencing hand. Standing up straighter and peering down his nose at his crew, a harsh glare settled on his features. "Is this the crew I sailed with to bring an end to the pirate wars in four days? Is this the crew I sailed with to defeat fleets a hundred ships strong?" Right before my eyes, a fire began to burn within the crew as they watched their leader.

"Aye, captain!" they chorused back to him. A smirk found its way to Jin's lips as he placed both of his hands firmly on the helm.

"My crew fears no fleet! It's those who dare cross us that fear retribution!"

"Aye!" the crew shouted.

"Now get ye'r scurvy covered backsides into gear! Lower those sails, get those fire barrels ready and load the cannons!" The crew instantly moved.

The cannons were loaded even faster than they were the first time. I couldn't help but gap at the connection the crew held with Jin.

How did he shake the fear from his crew with just a few sentences?

"First mate!" Startled, I shifted my stunned gaze to Jin. The smirk still present on his face made me feel secure for some reason as I mirrored his look.

"Yes, captain?"

"Are ye ready to give'em hell?"

"Aye, captain." He let out a bellowing laugh filled to the brim with mirth.

"The lass is already startin' to sound like part of the crew!" he lowered his gaze to me and smirked. "Let's do it!" Without warning,

Jin spun the wheel sharply to the left. "Drop anchor!"

"Drop anchor!" seconds later the anchor dropped, jerking the ship to a sudden halt. The ship slid in the water bringing the rear towards the fleet.

"Fire rear cannons!"

"Fire rear cannons!" The whizz of the cannon balls flying through the air blocked out all other sounds. I almost didn't hear Jin yell to drop the fire barrels. Seconds later after the command, the fire barrels were floating in the water, bobbing up and down in the waves trying their best to stay afloat in the chaos that desperately tried to take them under.

"Raise anchor!"

"Raise anchor!" This continued on for what seemed like hours.

Jin would tell me things to tell his crew to do- sometimes even screaming it out himself completely forgetting that I was there to do it for him. I didn't say anything considering I didn't even know what half the things I was saying meant. Besides, Jin has fought in hundreds of battles while my only experience was when Layne attacked the nomads. Even then, I didn't do anything more than fling a rock at a guy *hoping* it hit.

Throughout the grueling experience, Singer and Dove both actively helped the crew and even saved a couple of their lives. There were a few times in which the other ships were able to angle their guns in our direction before Jin could move us out of the way. The resulting damage could have killed almost half of the sailors if it weren't for Singer or Dove using their magic to mitigate the worst of it.

But how much longer can they keep it up?

"Jin," The sound of my voice was drowned out by cannon balls imbedding themselves into the side of the ship knocking everyone that wasn't holding something to the ground.

"Jin, we have to get out of here!" I shouted once the chaos settled slightly. Jin kept his gaze squarely on the enemy, assessing and reassessing what our next move should be.

Isn't it obvious? We're going to die if we stay here!

"Nay, we can't do that." My jaw nearly hit the floor as I stared at him in shock.

"Are you being serious?"

"We can't run."

"Are you really going to let your pride get us all killed?" I screamed back at him. I can feel my face heating up from anger, my fists going numb from how tightly I gripped the railing. "How can you be so-?"

"Even if I wanted to run," He spat, cutting me off, "there would be nothin' stoppin' Hawk and his fleet from enterin' Rosesea and conquerin' it." He finally turned his head to look at me, a grave look in his eyes. "With Clearapal *and* Rosesea under his command, where do ya think we can run next?" I opened my mouth, but paused.

He's right.

Swallowing hard, I nodded before turning back to the fleet still twelve ships strong. A sinking feeling started in the pit of my stomach.

How does he expect us to win when we've only done minimal damage to Hawk's ships?

"Then... what do we do now?" A smirk made an appearance on Jin's face as he gave me a sideways glance.

"Don't ever underestimate an ex-pirate capt'n!" he bellowed before turning to his men, a wide grin stretching across his lips.

"Prepare to board!"

"What?" the resounding shouts of excitement nearly drowned out my question.

Has he gone completely insane? How does he expect to infiltrate a ship when we can't even get close to one? His howl of laughter was my only answer as he spun the wheel sharply to the left causing us to veer straight for the open sea.

"Lower the sails!"

What is he planning?

From the corner of my eye, I could see one of the ships heading straight across our path. The crew were scrambling on deck desperately trying to slow the ship or turn it as fast as possible to avoid colliding with us.

Is he trying to ram it?

"Jin, what are you doing?" He didn't even look at me as heswung the wheel to the right.

"Brace for impact!" My breath hitched in my throat as I watched in silent horror as our ship closed in to the other.

The enemy vessel began to turn slightly as if they were going to dodge Jin's insane move, but Jin adjusted so the heads of the ships were aligned. Before anything could be done, the ships collided. The force of the blow made both boats bounce off the other before sliding alongside each other as if melding together. Neither us nor the other ship could move as shouts of panic and frustration filled the air from Hawk's men.

Jin's crew let out a loud battle cry as half of them began to raid the trapped boat. A bubble of panic filled the pit of my stomach when I saw Singer amongst them.

What is he thinking?!

"Ye shouldn't worry so much for ye'r friend." I turned my head slightly towards Jin. Although he was speaking to me, his eyes never left the battle raging just a few feet away from where we stood. "He's a smart lad and a spirited one at that! Look at him barrel through them scurvy miscreants!" The following laugh had me turning my attention to the battle.

Just like he said, Singer *was* practically steamrolling through the sailors that came at him. With his signature sword in hand, Singer batted away all those that came at him and sliced through a number of others who tried to attack him from behind. Within a minute, they had taken over the ship, throwing all of the survivors below deck.

"Impossoble- how can they take over an entire ship with only a few fighters?" I gaped.

"Never underestimate an ex-pirate, lass." Jin retorted, a wicked grin on his face as he unsheathed his sword. Thrusting it into the air, he let out a cry of victory which the men responded to tenfold. "Now let's take the rest!" The men responded in the same cheer before they began the work of pushing the ships apart.

When we were free, Jin began sailing us towards another ship close by. Meanwhile, the crew leapt into action, angling the cannons for a direct hit. From my peripheral, I saw the ship we invaded start sailing. Turning completely, I recognized the crew as our fighters that boarded. They skillfully took up their positions- raising sails, loading cannons and doing minor repairs were needed. Singer was at the helm ordering the men around as if it was second nature.

Since when does he know how to direct a ship?

The sound of wood breaking and cries of panic brought my attention back to the vessel we were facing off. The sight of it sinking to the bottom of the ocean had me floored. Weren't we just fighting them a few moments ago?

"Never underestimate the power of motivation." I turned my head to Jin to see him focusing solely on the remaining boats heading in our direction.

I blinked hearing the sounds of another ship going under and the cheers from Singer's crew behind us.

Seriously, what just happened?

Within ten minutes of commandeering a second vessel, seven ships were bombarded with cannon fire and sunk leaving only four badly damaged ships left. One of them left a trail of black smoke in their wake. Weren't we just getting our butts kicked? How did this even happen?

"They're retreatin', capt'n!" The corresponding roar of happiness radiating from both ships nearly deafened me. I could only stare slack jawed.

"This wouldn't be the first time we won when the odds were stacked so high against us." Glancing down, a boy who looked around my age beamed up at me as he rested a rifle against his shoulder. "Captain Jin is the best alive!" I blinked at him before the words processed in my head.

When has he let me down?

A wide smile spread across my lips as I nodded.

"You'd have to be crazy to doubt him!" The boy flashed me a final grin before heading back to his station.

I watched him retreat before glancing over to Jin. My smile dissipated at the growing alarm in his hardened eyes. Why does he have that look on his face? Didn't we win?

"Jin?" he didn't respond, he kept his attention locked on the horizon.

Dread filled my stomach as I hesitantly followed his gaze. The moment I saw what caused his unease, my blood ran cold.

Like earlier, the retreated ships came back with help... but this time they came ready to destroy us for good. Racing towards us was a fleet twenty-four vessels strong and armed to the teeth with more cannons than I dare count. The flagship was twice the size of ours as it towered over us even at a distance.

How many ships does Hawk have?

"Get to your stations, men!" Jin shouted in a harsh tone I've never heard from him before.

Glancing down at the crew, I could see why. The men looked utterly *terrified.* The dread on their faces said it all- not to mention how they just stood and gaped at the approaching enemy. The moment they heard their captain's voice; they got back into action. They moved faster than before, loading the cannons and raising the sails. Despite all of the preparations that the men did, there was one simple fact that I know plagued everyone on board.

"We'll never beat or run from a fleet this strong." I whispered in the salty breeze as it shuffled past.

The moment the words left my lips, two of the ships floated on either side of Singer's. Silence filled the air as horror closed my throat leaving me gasping for breath. A bright light covered the deck just as the ships let loose volley after volley of cannon fire. Chunks of wood exploded, launching high into the air. The waves thrashed violently as the ship practically disintegrated. As the echoes of the cannons began to fade, the remains of the ship sank beneath the waves. Only pieces of wood and bodies were left amongst the seafoam.

"Singer!" I screamed as the last piece of the ship fell below the ocean's surface.

A flash of light brought my attention to the deck below. As it died down, the men that were once on the sunken vessel stood with petrified looks frozen on their faces. Meanwhile, Singer was in the middle of the group, glaring at the two ships as they began to turn around.

"You just had to ruin my fun, didn't you?!" He shouted in clear annoyance.

The relief of seeing all of them alive was short lived as my eyes scanned over the crew. Despite defeating sixteen ships within the last hour, the sight of our commandeered ship getting destroyed within seconds decimated any form of hope or morale. They all knew the cold hard reality of what was about to happen.

We're all going to die.

"Hold on to ye'r courage and brace ye'rselves for battle!" Jin hollered, furiously turning the helm.

Then the cannon fire began.

Wave after wave of cannon fire racked the sides of the ship and destroyed nearly a quarter of the cannons. The men barely had enough time to fire back, and that's not even including the amount of men that were killed in the process. Jin tried his best to dodge at least some of the onslaught, but it wasn't nearly enough.

The ship is in near disrepair and the men reeked of fear and exhaustion. At this rate, we'll stand as much of a chance as Singer's ship.

Wait a minute, Singer!

Quickly looking through the crowd, my eyes zeroed in on his figure by a group of the cannons opposite to Dove as they tried their best to use their magic to keep them from being destroyed from the

fire.

"Singer!" I screamed over the mayhem.

Immediately, he turned his gaze up to me. His eyes darkened when they met mine, but in the next second, they went back to normal. An obnoxious look crossed his features as he looked at me expectantly. Taking in a deep breath, I gestured towards the ships tearing ours apart and, with pleading eyes, I focused solely on him.

"Do something!" I might have imagined it, but for a brief second, his eyes looked like they widened before he quickly looked away.

"Don't yell at me, you annoying stray!" he didn't look at me, opting to scan the crowd. His eyes seemed to zero in on something before he began to push through the crewmen.

Following his movements, I saw him make his way to Dove. Once he reached her, he grabbed her wrist. She turned prepared to strike whoever it was, but he said something to her before he dragged her behind him towards the front of the ship.

What is he doing?

My heart pounded in my chest as my knuckles turned white from my grip on the railing. With his back to me, I saw his hold around Dove's wrist tighten. He held a hand out towards the ships, his back tensing. For a couple of seconds, he didn't move. Suddenly, a bright light appeared above Hawk's fleet. Just as quickly as the light appeared, Singer thrusted his hand out to the side. The light grew brighter, blinding anyone who dared to look into it. I had to close my eyes and turn away from the sheer intensity of it. When the light died down, I took a peek. Where the fleet was supposed to be, was nothing but open waters. The only evidence that a massive fleet was ever there are gentle ripples.

Wow… who knew Singer was this *strong?*

Seeing movement in the corner of my eye had me turning my attention back towards Singer and Dove. Dove gave a violent sway before she fell to her hands and knees.

"Dove!" bolting down the steps to the deck, I sprinted as fast as I could. When I reached her, I dropped down next to her placing a hand on her back. "Dove, are you okay?" her breath came in rugged huffs as sweat dotted her skin. Inhaling deeply, she closed her eyes and nodded sharply.

"I'm fine." She shakily responded, slowly opening her eyes.

Giving her a once over anyway, I turned my attention to Singer. Peering up at him, my brows scrunched together as I watched his back.

Something isn't right. He would have at least turned around to poke at her about being an amateur. What's going on?

"Singer?" He tensed, showing that he heard me, but he still didn't face me. A bad feeling started in my throat as I swallowed.

"Singer, are you okay?" His shoulders slumped as he turned slightly. Before he could turn fully, his entire body went slack. With a loud thump, he hit the ground, his eyes closed. "Singer!" panic seized me as I moved closer to him.

He isn't dead...- right?

Quickly placing my ear to his chest, I could hear his heart beat loud and clear. Letting out a sigh of relief, I placed a hand to his forehead. It was a little warm to the touch but it's nothing too concerning. Besides a few cuts and bruises, he was perfectly healthy.

"He's fine, too." Dove started bringing my attention to her. She moved to her feet, wobbling slightly. When she was stable, she gave me a leveled look. "He's just exhausted. He channeled my magic along with his own to teleport the fleet elsewhere."

"But, Singer has used that spell before without side effects, why is it happening now? Shouldn't he be fine since he used both of your magic?" Dove blinked at me before rolling her eyes to gaze out across the calm sea.

"It may not be *that* draining of a spell when cast on a small group of people, but to do it against a fleet of that size... it takes a lot of magic. And I don't have the largest magic reserves."

In other words, Singer drained his magic to save us... again.

Slowly, I brought my gaze to look down at Singer's face. My eyes burned slightly as I grabbed his hand and placed it onto his chest.

"Thank you, Singer."

XI

It took us a while to get to the closest coastal region of Rosesea where the guard wasn't crawling. Unfortunately for our diminished supplies and horribly damaged ship, that region was on the shores of Rosemist. There are quite a few reasons why Rosemist is the *worst* place to be stranded when you have injured, hungry, and tired crew, but there are even more reasons why it's avoided in general.

First, Rosemist is plagued with high cliffs on its border with the sea. The exceptions are three small beaches barely large enough to accommodate one ship in their lagoons. Second, half of the land is usually covered in ice for half of the year. Lastly, it's the only country in Rosesea in which the faye are rumored to freely roam outside of the vast forest and terrorize the few people who dare to settle here.

What are we going to do now?

Taking a deep breath, I looked over to Singer's motionless form. Though it's been nearly four hours since the battle, Singer still hasn't woken up. It's like he drained himself of all of his magic leaving him a said shell of what he usually is. Jin assigned one of the intact rooms below deck for him to rest. He offered Dove the same, but she opted to help look after the other injured crewmen. I wanted to do the same, but I couldn't seem to leave Singer's side.

Biting my lower lip, anxiety took over me as I placed a hand against his cold cheek. He didn't even flinch. His breathing just continued its steady rhythm. A sigh broke through my lips as I withdrew my hand letting it hang loosely by my side. Watching him for a few more seconds, I swallowed the lump forming in my throat.

"I'm going to go see if the camp is ready. If it is, then I'll get some of the crew to move you there. Alright you heartless fairy?"

Nothing- not even a twitch of his brow or a grimace touched his lips.

Now I'm really getting worried- what if using that much magic at once sent him into a coma? What are we supposed to do without him?

Shaking my head furiously to rid myself of those terrible thoughts, I readjusted his blanket. After one more once over, I turned and left the room, closing the door silently behind me.

Walking through the narrow hallway, I could almost convince myself that everything was fine. That we didn't almost die at sea. However, by the time I made it up the stairs and onto the deck, reality hit like a slap in the face. Massive holes littered the sides of the ship. Chunks of the bow were blown off leaving behind charred marks. The scent of blood mixed with sea salt burned my nose. Some of the surviving crew members were removing whatever fallen debris they could. Given the worn out, hollow look in their eyes, they were also the ones who gathered the dead bodies.

How often will that happen until this is over?

If this is what's going to happen after every battle with Hawk then I'd rather end this on my own. I'd rather steal a boat and have Hawk chase me for the rest of my life. I'd rather run for the rest of my life than put more innocent people in graves. But then again, would that even work? Would Hawk spare all these people just because I ran off on my own?

No.

"The lass has finally graced us with her presence!" Turning, Jin strolled towards me, an easygoing grin on his face. Placing his hands on his hips, he regarded me with kind eyes. With the way he's acting, it's like we didn't just get decimated.

Maybe it's because he knew we'd make it out?

"So, what brought ya out of ye'r hollow, hmm?" I blinked at him before gazing overboard towards the shore. Four large tents stood at a safe distance from the waves. Off to the right, a handful of men were digging.

At least we'll be able to bury the ones that weren't lost at sea…

"I wanted to check if camp was ready." I started turning my attention back to Jin. "Can we take Singer to the medical tent?" Jin straightened as he looked out towards the campsite.

"Aye, we can bring the faye to camp. They've finished buryin' the dead and the injured have already been tended to. I'll send some men fer your friend." I nodded silently. He gave my shoulder a firm pat before waving over his shoulder at a couple of men. "Don't worry, lass. Yer friend is too stubborn to be taken out this easily." I swallowed the lump forming in my throat. Lowering my gaze, I felt my eyes burn.

"If... if I asked you for the truth, would you tell me?"

"Of course."

"Do you regret helping me? Or, do you regret making a deal with my father to begin with?" His grin lost some of its cheerfulness, but he turned away before I could fully see it leave. He removed his hand from my shoulder to fold them over his chest.

"I know a lot about regret, lass. But," he tilted his head back to me, a tired smile touching his lips. "I've never fought fer somethin' I wasn't willin' to die for. Neither have my men."

"But-"

"Ya asked me fer the truth, right, lass?" He fully turned to me again. I nodded, a weight crushing my chest. "People die in battle- even more so in war. If any of my men weren't willin' to take the risk, they wouldn't have been onboard. The only way they'd regret stayin', is if there wasn't anything worth fightin' fer. So, is protectin' their homes-families from a bilge-sucking rapscallion hellbent on stirrin' up chaos worth it?" meeting his steady gaze, I would be an idiot not to believe him. The corner of my lips upturned.

"Is that your way of telling me not to die?" He chuckled softly.

"Aye- that would be the point." He observed me for a moment before ruffling my hair. I squeaked, swatting away his hands. He laughed again. "I have some more work to do. Try not to sulk too much." With that, he walked away. I watched him leave while trying to fix my curls.

I swear- he acts more like an older brother than a pirate.

"Miss?" whirling on the balls of my feet, I saw one of the men standing a few feet away. He attempted a gentle smile, but the grief and sheer exhaustion shined through the façade.

"What is it?"

"We are about to move Mr. Singer. Would you like to come with us?" I nodded before following him towards the ramp leading down towards the beach.

Just as we reached it, two men emerged from below deck holding a stretcher. Singer lay motionless on top of it, a blanket wrapped tightly around him. The men carefully carried him down the ramp before immediately heading towards the medical tent.

If I mortally wound his pride, will that wake him up?

"Miss?" My attention turned back to the crewman, his brow scrunched together in concern. Not trusting myself to keep a steady tone, I swallowed hard and descended down the ramp. Heading straight for the medical tent, I couldn't help but notice about a dozen large mounds of dirt, freshly tossed back into place with small wooden planks marked with a name.

How many more graves will there be before this is over?

"Jayde." Slowly, I peeled my eyes away from the new graveyard to see Dove standing before me. Her face was still sickly pale and her shoulders slacked slightly, but she still held the air of mystery and power that she always has.

That means there's no reason to be too concerned, right? "Dove, are you alright?" She smiled, crossing her arms.

"There's no reason for you to worry. I can assure you I'm fine." I nodded before glancing past her towards the tent.

"Can you say the same for Singer?" the smile nearly disappeared from her lips as she gazed over her shoulder.

"He'll be fine. He just needs to get a bit more rest before he wakes up."

What if he stays like this?

My heart squeezed uncomfortably. I could only hum in acknowledgment before walking by her and into the tent.

Hanging sheets separated each patient giving them a little privacy. Scanning the room, my eyes zeroed in on the rear of the tent where the curtain was drawn. Singer lay on the small cot breathing deeply. Silently, I walked over to his bed side, sitting down on theedge of the cot as I watched him sleep.

Maybe if I annoy him, he'll wake up?

"I'm going to go help the men repair the ship. Will you be alright here?" I turned away from Singer to face Dove. A sigh broke through my lips.

"Go ahead. I'll be fine." She nodded before spinning around and walking out. Moving my gaze back towards Singer, a frown settled on my lips. "You better not be faking to get out of helping." No reaction. "If I find out you're faking I'll make you regret it." His breathing kept its steady pace. I was about to say something else, when a glowing white light floated past my face and landed on Singer's chest before fluttering off.

A pixie?

"Your heart's in the right place, but it'll take more than that to wake him." My eyes widened as I whirled around.

Bellatrix? What is she doing here?

A gentle smile formed on the fairy queen's lips. Her gaze shifted from my bewildered face down to Singer. She let out a soft hum before looking over her shoulder. Without having to utter a single word, Apple appeared by her side staring up at her with pure adoration.

"My queen?"

"Tend to our fallen comrade while I have a talk with our friend." Apple nodded enthusiastically before bounding to Singer. She knelt beside Singer taking his hand in hers. She closed her eyes and began to mouth a chant. Within seconds, both of their hands began to let off a light blue glow.

"What are you doing?"

"She's restoring his magic reserves." Bellatrix easily explained before walking to me, the pixies I didn't realize that were surrounding her created a glowing pathway. She stopped in front of me holding out a hand. "Come. Let's leave the injured to rest in peace and have our chat in a more secluded setting." I nodded dumbly, placing my hand in hers.

Warmth spread throughout my entire body when our hands touched. The stress melted away as a feeling of pure elation took over. It's like I was standing next to a fire on a cold winter night. Like nothing in the world could harm me. Like no evil exists.

No wonder her fairies are so obsessed with her. She's like the embodiment of happiness.

She must have noticed how I felt based on the knowing smile gracing her lips. Turning on her heels, she led me out of the tent and into the middle of camp. We headed towards the largest tent- the one meant to hold everyone- when Bellatrix suddenly paused. Giving her a curious glance, I opened my mouth to question her when a dark purple light flitted across my peripheral vision.

Turning towards it, I nearly gasped at the hundreds of dark purple pixies drifting slowly creating a pathway leading into the forest.

Aren't those Alastar's pixies?

On cue, the fairy king himself waltzed from the depths of the forest. A devilish smirk on his face and Elah by his side.

"Bellatrix! How long has it been since the last time we've seen each other?" he greeted, stopping a few feet away from us. A discontented hum sounded next to me as Bellatrix dropped my hand.

Surprisingly, that cozy feeling lingered.

"Since you announced your queen." She retorted, raising a perfectly sculpted brow at him. Tension filled the air nearly suffocating me. As if sensing it, Dove emerged from the ship walking purposefully down the ramp towards us. When he eyes landed on Bellatrix, she immediately bowed.

"My queen." Bellatrix smiled brightly at her, waving away her show of respect.

"You've done your job very well, my little Dove." A dust of pink covered Dove's cheeks as she quickly turned away. Bellatrix let out a soothing laugh before motioning Dove to stand by me.

Obediently, Dove moved to my side. Once that was done, Bellatrix turned her attention back to Alastar and Elah, a frown now settled on her lips.

What's going on between those two?

"Is this some sort of lover's quarrel?" I whispered leaning close to Dove. She looked taken aback at my question as she raised a brow.

"What do you mean?"

"I mean- she's the fairy queen and he's the fairy king. So, doesn't that mean that they're supposed to be together or something? Isn't that why Elah and Bellatrix hate each other?" she blinked twice at me before understanding seemed to dawn on her.

"Jayde, the fairy king and queen are siblings."

My lips formed an 'O' shape as I lowered my head to hide the blush that tainted my cheeks.

Well, that's not *embarrassing.*

"So, Bellatrix," I spoke quickly, turning completely towards her. The fairy queen glanced down at me, a soft smile on her lips. "What are you doing here?" She raised an amused brow as her smile widened. My cheeks burned as I raised my hands defensively. "Not that I'm unhappy you're here, but-"

"There's no need for you to be nervous, Jayde." My eyes widened as she let out a light giggle. She reached out a delicate hand and cupped my cheek. "I'll explain everything in due time, but fornow, we need to make sure everyone is taken care of."

Like Singer.

"Apple will be able to make him wake up, won't she?"

"I have no doubt. That boy's actions may make him seem reckless, but he's a sly fairy."

"He *is* reckless, but what does that have to do with you being here now?"

"That foolishness," Alastar started, the white lines running through his eyes blazing in amusement, "was the point." Bellatrix glanced towards him, a blank look on her face before a sigh broke through her lips. Letting her hand slip from my face, she slid it to my back.

"Let's move somewhere more fitting to chat." I nodded, my body feeling lighter from her touch. She gently pushed me in the direction of Jin's tent. Without hesitation, Bellatrix pushed back the flaps gesturing for me to enter first. I walked in followed closely by Bellatrix, Alastar and Elah.

The room is designed almost identically to Jin's captain's quarters. There was a large desk in the back of the room with a few papers and writing utensils scattered on top. In the middle of the room lay an assembly of large pillows with only six chairs settled directly in front of the desk.

Did Jin have all of these supplies locked under the ship or something?

"Alright," Bellatrix began, elegantly gliding towards the desk and settling herself onto one of the chairs. Her multi-colored eyes rested on me, a warm smile on her lips. "What is it that you want to know first?" I blinked at her as Alastar and Elah brushed past me, taking a seat next to Bellatrix.

"Why are you here?" Alastar's eyes brightened with amusement, but before he could say anything, the flaps to the tent flew open. Jin stood in all his glory, his eyes scanning over the occupants. His scrutinizing gaze lingered on Alastar for a second longer, but he turned towards me without a word to the fairy king.

"I'm surprised ye aren't in the medical tent lookin' after ye'r friend. Ya didn't leave his side all the way here."

"I was planning to, but then they showed up." Jin visibly stiffened.

"Aye." He muttered making his way towards the desk. Even when he sat down, his back was ramrod straight. His eyes never once traveled anywhere near Alastar's direction. "Well, that begs the question, what are ya doin' in my camp?" Bellatrix glanced between Alastar's amused face and Jin's tense posture for a moment, raising a perfect brow.

"Captain Jin, it's been a while since the last time we met." Alastar casually greeted leaning back comfortably. Slowly, Jin shifted his gaze to Alastar, his face uncharacteristically void of all emotion.

"Alastar, king of all dark faye. To what do I owe ye'r unexpected visit?" The grin on Alastar's face only grew.

"It seems I have business with the last Henryk, but there's no reason why I would be opposed to sharing friendly dialogue with an old acquaintance." Jin's jaw tightened, his eyes watching Alastar's movements like a hawk. The fairy king let out a deep rumbling laugh in response. I can practically see Jin's hidden hands twitch towards his pistols. "I also wanted to give you some good news about your little friend Parsley." Something flashed across Jin's eyes.

"What happened?" Alastar lazily shrugged.

"She's alive and well, but from what I have seen, she doesn't have any memory of the life she previously led." Just like that, Jin's shoulders slumped and the stress lines that formed on his face the moment he saw Alastar disappeared.

"How is that good news?" Bellatrix piped in giving the fairy king a hard frown. Said man merely glanced over at her, mischief shining in his eyes.

"I did say *some* good news, didn't I?"

"What is good about that?"

"Isn't knowing she's alive and healthy good enough." Bellatrix's frown deepened, the dark purple ring in her eyes flickering like a fire.

This isn't looking good.

"You didn't have to tell him that." I stated. Alastar turned his bemused gaze to me. He crossed his legs, the white lines in his eyes dancing in amusement.

"And why not, my dear?"

"Because it's cruel. You know that Jin wants to be reunited with her and you're throwing it in his face-" Alastar raised a finger.

The bored look on his face was enough of a warning to silence me. After all of the stories I've heard, there's no way I'd dare over step boundaries with him. Push them? Of course. But never cross.

"Or is it?" my eyes widened as he lowered his finger back to his lap. "Isn't it better that he knows now instead of wasting time seeking her out and then realizing it was useless? Which do you think would have destroyed him more?" I pursed my lips. Elah let out a sound of approval, placing a hand on Alastar's.

"At least the peasant can rest assured his beloved isn't being held back anymore."

How can she say something so horrible?!

I opened my mouth to shout- to scream at her to take it back, but the hand that Jin raised made me bite my tongue.

"Leave it be, lass. No need ranglin' over bitter history."

What?

I wanted to tell him that they couldn't get away with being so cruel, but then again how could I? After all, it is his history that we're talking about. What right do I have to make a big deal about it if he doesn't?

Besides, I would feel the same way if someone kept trying to speak about Aric.

Just the thought of him had my hand snaking into my pocket where his dormant soul lay. The feel of it in my hand comforted me. *There's still a chance you'll come back to me.*

Reluctantly, I kept my mouth shut. I settled on sending Elah a nasty glare.

"Now then, if you're finished angering our allies," Bellatrix started shooting Alastar a look from the corner of her eye, "why don't we answer the question everyone has on their mind?" Alastar made a noise in the back of his throat. Closing his eyes, he leaned his head back until it touched the chair.

"The question on why we're here, I presume?"

"Yes." Bellatrix turned her gaze to me. She gestured for me to come closer. Without thinking much of it, I walked to her, taking a seat in the chair beside her. She placed an arm loosely around my shoulders in a comforting manner. "Now, to answer your question.

We're here because of Singer and Dove."

"What- why?! You said you wouldn't help! Both of you explicitly said-"

"We won't intervene until Hawk has proven to be a threat to our kind." Alastar piped in.

"So, what's changed?"

"Hawk's attack on Jin's ship." An impish twinkle entered Bellatrix's eyes as she gazed down at me.

"Why would that change anything?"

"When Hawk attacked the ship, he attacked Dove and Singer."

"And seeing how both of them are under the rule of Bellatrix, it's a direct declaration of war against, not only her, but me." I raised a brow at Alastar's signature grin.

"But why would you care if Hawk declares war on Bellatrix?"

A bemused chuckle left his lips causing my cheeks to burn slightly.

That wasn't that dumb of a question... right?

"Because, if he's bold enough to attack her, then what's stopping him from going after me next?"

That's reasonable, but I still don't get why they're here now.

As far as I can tell, nothing has changed. Hawk's focus is solely on killing *me.* He hasn't gone after any faye thus far. The only ones he's shown any aggression towards is Singer and Dove-

And they're servants of Bellatrix!

I barely restrained myself from face palming. How could I forget that detail about my traveling companions?

Then again, with how those two act, you can easily forget they serve anyone other than their egos.

"So this means... you two have no choice but to get involved?" I asked slowly, my eyes drifting between Alastar's teasing smirk and Bellatrix's amused grin.

"I'm surprised you didn't think about that until now. You three were bound to fall in between Hawk's crosshairs. It was only a matter of time until we were dragged in." Alastar laughed, sitting straighter in his chair.

I have a feeling he won't let me live this down.

Silently cursing myself for forgetting such an important fact, I turned my head away from the both of them.

"It slipped my mind that they are her servants. I mean, they don't act like any servants of royalty that I've ever seen." I grumbled crossing my arms over my chest. God, I can practically see how red my cheeks are!

"I don't blame you for it, darling." Bellatrix cooed, tightening her grip around me. Turning back to her, I can feel the warmth she radiated just by looking into her eyes. "As monarchs, we rarely call upon our subjects unless it involves dire situations."

"Like a war?" The joke wasn't lost on her as the white and pink rings of her eyes brightened in amusement.

"Exactly." She shifted her gaze from me, allowing her eyes to look at every occupant in the room.

"But I still don't get it. If you were going to get involved anyway, why not help from the start? Why wait until we almost died?" Bellatrix hummed thoughtfully.

"That's something we can discuss later." Giving my shoulder a squeeze, she leveled me with a small smile. "Now, let's focus on solving the biggest problem."

"Which is?" A grim line covered her lips.

"Hawk's inevitable arrival to kill you."

"Oh," I dumbly responded, lowering my head to look at my hands in my lap. "But he's not that big of a deal with you guys involved, right?"

"To us, yes. To you, not so much." Alastar laughed. Before I could respond, the tent's flaps flew open.

"Seriously- I can't leave you for five minutes before you're spouting nonsense again, you foolish stray."

I've never been happier to hear that obnoxious voice.

"That would sound like nonsense to a nitwit." I retorted, trying to fight the smile forming on my face. "By the way, good morning, sleeping beauty." Singer grumbled something under his breath before marching into the tent. Grabbing a chair, he placed it on the side of Jin's desk directly in front of me. Sitting down, he crossed his arms and propped his ankle on his right knee.

"I take offense to being called *only* beautiful when I'm clearly much more stunning, but I'll let it slide. Clearly, you need some much needed education on the faye monarchy." I rolled my eyes.

Drama queen.

I leaned back in my chair, settling him with an expectant gaze.

It couldn't help to hear him out, could it?

"Then enlighten me."

"I don't think anyone can enlighten a moron like you, but I digress."

"Said the pot to the kettle." A smirk formed on his lips before he cleared his throat.

"Contrary to what you may think, the monarchs can't just snap their fingers and an army appears. They have to rally their forces together and *then* bring them to the battlefield which, if you haven't realized, will take some time." I raised a brow turning my gaze up to Bellatrix who looked at me with bemused eyes.

"Can't you guys, like, send out a signal or something?" The burst of laughter brought my attention back to Singer, a glare on my face.

Can he last a second without being sarcastic?

"What- do you think all of us are in the same place? I mean, come on- didn't you notice the lack of neighbors at my house"

"In that case," I started through gritted teeth, focusing back on Bellatrix, "how long will it take?" She hummed contemplatively before turning to Alastar.

"I'll be ready in three days." The fairy king snorted, raising a dismissive hand.

"I can match that."

What- three days?! Hawk will be blowing us to bits by then!

In a panic, I snapped my head to Singer, a pleading look shining on my face.

"How far away did you send Hawk's army?" He didn't speak for several seconds. Shrugging, he relaxed back into his chair.

"Considering the abysmal level of magic I could pull from that amateur, I got us an extra day. If I had more power, I could have sent them further." Fear took hold of me as my eyes widened.

"How are we supposed to hold off Hawk and his army for two days? We were nearly wiped out in less than two hours this time!"

"In that case," everyone turned to face Alastar, his eyes shining with mirth, "now you know what you're up against."

Is he serious!

"In the meantime," picking up my jaw from the floor, I slowly moved my eyes to Bellatrix, her own sparkling with encouragement, "you will have the support of my three personal fairies and my nomads." A grunt was heard from the fairy king as he rubbed the back of his neck leaning forward.

"Geez, you just have to be the little show off, huh Bellatrix?"

Said woman merely brushed his comment off with a flick of her wrist. Alastar huffed. "Then, I guess I have no choice." He leaned back in his chair crossing his arms. "I'll match that by sending some agents I can scrape together. However," My eyes narrowed as his gaze darkened, giving me an uncanny harsh stare, "you need to come up with a proper strategy to make sure we're not fighting a losing battle.

I won't throw my subjects into the lion's den if it's not worth it."

"I promise." I responded in a daze.

Who knew the fairy king, of all people, would be the one to lecture me on the value of someone's life?

"Good!" He exclaimed practically jumping from his seat, a wide grin that reeked of mischief plastered on his face, "I'll see you in three days!" Turning slightly, he held out a hand towards Elah who, surprisingly, stayed silent throughout the entire meeting. Maybe Alastar told her to let him handle the negotiations?

Or maybe he told her not to speak to me because of how our last meeting went? Not to mention Bellatrix is here…

"I suppose we've discussed everything." Gracefully rising to her feet, Bellatrix took my hand in hers giving it a light squeeze. The warmth that came with it practically smothered me. "Don't worry, my little Jayde. Everything will turn out as it should." Oddly enough, I feel comforted. Even though the monarchs don't guarantee that *everything* will turn out right, they do give me the hope that most of it will.

"Yeah, see you soon." The fairy queen gave me one last smile before letting my hand slip through her grasp. Turning her back, she made her way towards the exit with a poised gait. Pausing at the flaps, she looked over her shoulder at Alastar.

"I trust I can count on you not to be late to the battle, right Alastar?" Said man smirked, holding his hands out wide, he gestured to himself.

"Aren't I known to arrive just in time?" Bellatrix let out a small chuckle.

"Of course."

Is it just me or is Elah's face getting redder by the second?

Throughout the short exchange between the two monarchs, Elah's face turned from a pale pink to full blown scarlet as if she's barely keeping her anger in check.

"Instead of worrying about what *we* are doing,"

Here we go.

"Make sure *you* don't send a bunch of useless fodder."

Bellatrix's face went still, her smile slowly slipping from her lips.

Before Alastar could act, Bellatrix was already practically nose to nose with her. Elah's eyes widened minutely, her back stiff.

"Such strong words from a *fragile* little toy." Raising a perfectly smooth hand, Bellatrix gripped Elah's jaw. Her sharp nails digging into Elah's skin. "It would be a shame if you *broke* during the skirmish. You're only here because of luck, after all." Bellatrix's grip tightened, the slightest amount of blood making an appearance just below her finger. "Without him, you know as well as I do where you would *still* be." Something flashed across Elah's eyes, but it was gone before I could get a good look.

Was that fear or hatred?

"You should learn how to bow to your superiors without getting on your knees." Just as the final syllable was spoken, Bellatrix vanished before our eyes leaving behind the remnants of her pixies' soft white light.

If she didn't explode before, then she's definitely going to now.

"As much as I would love to stay here and continue our little chat," Alastar started, his eyes never leaving Elah's burning face, "I do believe it's time for us to go." Glancing up to look him in the eye, Elah stiffly nodded before she seemed to drop through the floor disappearing in an instant. The second she was out of sight, a deep sigh left Alastar. "I can't believe *I'm* the most civil amongst the three of us." Turning his head to look between the rest of us, a playful smirk formed on his lips. "It's been a pleasure." His eyes paused on me, his smile widening. "See you on the battlefield." Looking towards Jin, his eyes flashed. "It's been wonderful catching up."

"Ye should leave before ya find ye'r self in trouble, mate." Jin gritted out through his teeth. Alastar let out a bellowing laugh.

"Touché, Captain Jin." With that said, he disappeared in a flash of purple pixie light. The minute the light faded from the room, I could feel life returning to my two companions as they visibly relaxed.

"Are they that intimidating to be around?" I whispered.

"Did you not feel their aura? My skin is still crawling!" Singer admonished leaning forward onto his knees letting out a soft huff.

"Aye, and it doesn't help that the king is an insane bastard." Jin piped in, running a hand down his face. He let out a shaky breath before leaning over his desk, folding his arms on top of it. "Now then, why don't we get our little helpers in here to talk about the upcomin' battle we will be facin', aye?"

"Roger that, Captain." Singer responded, tilting his head towards the flaps of the tent. "After all, those four *have* been eavesdropping since the beginning." Just as he finished speaking, the flaps flew open allowing Fawn, Cherry, Apple and Dove to walk inside.

"We don't eavesdrop, boy. We simply stay close to our queen." Fawn haughtily defended, dropping into the seat that Alastar occupied.

"I think we were mostly *just* eavesdropping." Cherry stated, sitting down next to me. Her peach-colored eyes flashed with amusement. "Besides, there's nothing in this world that our queen can't handle. We're merely her shields and swords that fight so she doesn't have to."

"Spoken like a true poet." Fawn spat back at her, but the look in her eyes was anything but malicious. Cherry nodded at her before turning her eyes to me.

"How have you been fairing? Have you been enjoying keeping your brother company?" My jaw tightened as I turned away.

"Why don't we focus on the task our queen has given us?"

Apple interrupted sitting down on the ground in front of Jin's desk. Cherry stuck her tongue out at the elder girl while Fawn merely turned away with an unamused expression.

One minute they're acting like they're older than all of us and the next they're like five-year-olds! What's the deal with them anyway?

"Right." I mumbled, turning my head to face everyone in the room. "What *are* we going to do?"

"Excellent question, stray. Do you have anything to contribute or are you going to leave that to us?" Ignoring Singer's bait into an argument, I kept my attention solely on the other five occupants.

If you ignore him, he'll go away… but then again, this is Singer we're dealing with.

"There's nothing complicated about it." Fawn retorted, rising from her seat. "Apple and Captain Jin are going to take out as many of their ships as they can before they reach shore. When the remaining ships dock, Cherry will lead a firing squad to pick off as many of them as they can before they invade the villages. Those still left will be met with combat in the streets with myself, Singer, and Dove leading."

"Where do you think this battle is going to be taking place?

There aren't any villages for miles."

"That's because," I turned to Cherry as she examined her nails with disinterest, "if Hawk is smart, which- to a certain extent- he is, then he will be heading to Jancliff."

"Why there?"

"I don't know, stray. Maybe because it's the best place to draw you out?" This time, I couldn't help but shoot Singer a nasty glare before turning my attention to Fawn. Her gaze felt cold and yet it held no emotion- almost like a statue.

"Alright, then in your grand plan what am I supposed to do?"

"You'll stay at the rear and aid the medical team."

Are you serious?

My eyes hardened as I shot from my seat.

"I won't cower while people die protecting me!"

"It is that precise reason why you're staying in the back." She snapped, taking a threatening step towards me. "Don't forget the true reason as to *why* Hawk is coming in the first place and don't forget what will happen *if* he accomplishes it."

The end of the world.

I lowered my head as a sinking feeling filled my gut. I already know all of that. That if I die, then everything that's been sacrificed will be in vain. Just the thought of the fresh grave mounds lying outside is enough to make tears sting the back of my eyes.

Swallowing hard, I shoved the feeling aside, shutting my eyes tightly.

"Fine." I gruffly stated, not even bothering to open my eyes to witness the smug look that will no doubt be on her face.

I don't think I'll be able to bite my tongue if I see it.

"If that matter is settled," I slowly opened my eyes in time to see her moving to Jin's desk where a large map of the world lay, "let's get to planning out our movements, shall we? It's going to be hellish tomorrow."

XII

"Are you ready?" I sighed heavily for the millionth time today. Turning slightly, I looked into Dove's soft gaze as she glanced down at me.

"Can anyone really be prepared for war knowing they're outnumbered, outmatched, and outgunned?" Slowly, I rose from the ground, dusting my breeches. Dove turned away in contemplation.

"I guess not." Returning her attention to me, a gentle smile touched her lips. "But one can never give up hope." I grunted, walking towards the edge of town towards the medical tents.

Being back in Redmage is... surreal. All able-bodied villagers have joined our ranks including the nomads who were already here when we arrived. The rest of them were sent further back to Fallbell through a magical path designed for us to make a quick escape if needed.

Given how small our army is right now, we're going to have to.

Surprisingly, the Guard has also joined us. Turns out, the guards we saw previously were preemptively sent here by Bellatrix. Apparently, she had already anticipated Redmage would be turned into a battleground. So, using her people in the guard, she made sure all civilians that couldn't fight were evacuated while anyone who would stayed - hence the sketchy circumstances we saw before. It also explained why Dove and Cadian didn't know. It was a covert operation meant to throw off any spies working for Hawk. Who knew Bellatrix's power stretched out to humans as well? Or at least, I *did* think that until Dove explained that all of the guard with us - nearly two hundred strong- are all nymphs.

Then again, that doesn't really surprise me anymore.

"Jayde?" Snapping my head around, my eyes widened slightly at the sight of Ginger walking towards me.

"Ginger, it's good to see you." A small smile flashed across her lips before it vanished, being replaced by a grim line.

Is she anxious too?

"Where are you stationed in Fawn's grand plan?" She stared at me for a moment before her eyes drifted off.

"I'm part of the final line." Her voice sounded hollow and empty.

What's wrong with her?

"What do you think... what do you think is going to happen?" her eyes sluggishly came to focus back on me. Silence hung around us for what felt like hours.

"Are you afraid?"

"I'm not afraid of Hawk."

"But you *are* afraid of the outcome, aren't you?" I opened my mouth but closed it quickly.

Can't argue against that.

No matter how monstrous he is, Hawk is still human. A bullet can kill him just as easily as it can me. The only thing I fear is *what* he might do. *Who* he might kill just to get the power of the jewel. That's what makes my blood run cold. But if I'm being truly honest - if I *really* face the truth- what keeps me up at night is the future. The unknown fallout once everything is said and done. The ending that follows if we win. I'm not a faye. I can't stay in the forest forever. It's also not like I can return to Clearapal. Even if I wanted to go back, what would I do? My father already ensured that we were reported dead so it's not like any of our family assets will be there. Plus, what would happen if Aric awakened then? Would he be safe in Clearapal?

Would he be safe amongst the villagers in Roseasea?

Will he even remember me?

My heart clenched painfully.

I don't fear Hawk, but I do *fear what will happen if I live.*

"There's no need for you to be afraid, Jayde." My eyes focused back on Ginger, a comforting smile on her face. I guess something in my eyes tipped her off that I didn't believe her. She grabbed my hand, twisting it until my palm faced up.

"What are you doing?" She grinned in response. Taking her index finger, she traced the lines on my palm letting out a soft hum.

"You have a complex fate. The lines on your palms say a great strife will come your way, but if you can endure it, you'll live in everlasting serenity with the ones you love the most." Glancing between her and my palm, a tiny, sincere grin began to spread across my lips.

What a steaming pile.

"Are you sure that's what my palm says?"

"Who knows," she began releasing my hand, "but do you want to know what I think?" Repressing the urge to laugh, I nodded. "Though the future may end in blood, it can also end in peace." My smile dropped, but the weight lessened a little.

Is it alright to hold out hope everything will be ok?

"Who would've thought *you* would be the one to quote our queen?" Dove giggled approaching us. Ginger's face fell, her eyes dropping to the ground.

"She told us that before assigning us to Redmage five months ago..." her voice trailed off as it began to shake the slightest bit.

Oh. That's when Patrick...

"I'm sorry for your loss." Dove whispered. She tapped her lips with her finger before bringing them to her forehead. Ginger copied her before the two hooked their pinkies together, raising them slowly before breaking apart.

"Thank you." Ginger breathed, squeezing her eyes closed. "How's Karlie?" Her eyes opened with a slight glimmer. Focusing on me, a gentle smile appeared. From over her shoulder, Ginger gave me a grateful nod.

That seemed to take her mind off of Patrick. At least, for the time being.

"She's doing well. It seems like she's growing taller every day."

"Where is she?"

"She's in Fallbell with the others." I nodded, giving her a playful smile.

"She's properly hassling everyone to buy bread." A light laughter surrounded us before it abruptly stopped. Keeping my eyes on Ginger, a faraway look glazed over her features.

"I wonder... what will happen to her if I don't make it?"

Taken aback, I shook it off as a small frown formed on my face.

"There's no need to worry about that because there's no way that'll happen."

"Not everyone comes home from war, Jayde." Her eyes grew glassy as her head lowered slightly. "No matter how much you might want them to."

"Ginger-"

"I want you to promise me something." Shocked, I only nodded dumbfounded. "If I die, please make sure Karlie is taken care of."

What?

"Why are you asking me? There's definitely better-"

"Because despite what you may believe, you are the only one here that's most likely to live." The look in her eyes was desperate - close to pleading.

How can I say no?

"Yeah... ok. I promise." Her shoulders went slack as her face softened.

"Thank you, Jayde." I swallowed hard.

I have a horrible feeling about this.

Glancing in Dove's direction, I can tell she isn't happy about the situation. Her lips were pulled into a deep frown, her eyes narrowed discontentedly at Ginger.

"Ginger, is that you?" We both turned to see Cadian marching towards us- a wide friendly grin plastered on his face.

Thank goodness he's here- I don't think I can take this depressing talk anymore.

"It feels like ages since the last time I've seen you!" His grin took on a sheepish tone as he rubbed the back of his neck.

"From what I've heard, I can understand that." We all enjoyed a light laugh. As Cadian's eyes landed on Ginger, his face took on a more serious nature.

"Listen, I'm sorry I wasn't able to say this months ago, but I'm-"

"You don't have to say anything." Ginger cut in, grabbing hold of his hand. Cadian looked stunned for a moment before it quickly melted away. Giving her a slight nod. "Besides, there's no time for getting distracted by the past."

Not if the past is keeping you from moving on into the future.

Before I could say anything, a loud horn echoed in the air around us, vibrating through my very core.

"He's here." Cadian whispered. Dove, Ginger, and Cadian looked at each other before nodding silently. My heart hammered in my chest as all of them turned towards me.

"Get ready, Jayde." I could barely register Dove's words as I nodded. My lungs contracted violently as I broke out into a sprint towards the medical tent.

This is it.

Everything grew still. The sun, halfway through its descent towards the horizon cast an orange glow upon the land that will soon become a battleground.

One can dream that we won't have any casualties.

My heart pounded in my ears at the thought. I know there's no way we can avoid casualties- I've been told many times by too many people to be able to believe otherwise- but what if I find a body and it's someone that I know? What if someone stumbles into the medical tent with Dove's bloodied body slung over their shoulders? What if it's Ginger- or Cadian- or Jin – *or Singer?*

Squeezing my eyes closed, I banished the thoughts from my mind. This is not the time nor the place to be thinking about such things.

"Jayde?" I turned to see the head doctor, Charlotte- a beautiful woman with dark hair and shining brown eyes- walking towards me. She placed a gentle hand on my shoulder, shooting me a comforting smile. "There's no need for you to worry. We have the strongest beings in the world on our side- there's nothing on this Earth that can bring them down." I swallowed hard, turning my gaze downward.

"I used to think the same thing... then I got shot." Charlotte looked stunned for a moment before understanding seemed to dawn on her. Her lips formed a stiff line as her hand slipped from me.

"Faye always learn from their mistakes- and they never allow for it to happen a second time." I opened my mouth to say something, but the distant sound of cannon fire cut me off.

They're here.

My heart pounded in my ears as all eyes turned towards the horizon. The sky was lit with flashes of red, orange, and yellow followed by deafening bangs that shook the ground. There has to be at least a hundred cannons being fired from the constant flow of explosions and the never ending flares.

How many more ships does Hawk have?

The ringing of a church bell cut me off. Dread settled in the pit of my stomach as a lump formed in my throat.

They've reached Jancliff.

"Everyone, get ready for the arrival of the injured!" Charlotte commanded, snapping most of the staff out of their daze. No matter how hard I try, I just can't tear my eyes away from the battle slowly making its way towards us.

After all, they are coming to kill me.

“How long will it take before they get here?” Charlotte paused for only a second to glance towards the horizon. The echoes of gunshots and canons grew closer by the second. Her eyes widened by a fraction before she schooled her features into a professional mask.

“Two hours.” Was her response before she was back to ordering the nurses to move faster. My heart skipped a beat, my breath catching in my throat in a single painful inhale. Only two hours - it should take them at least four to get here!

How are we supposed to survive for two days?

“What are we supposed to do when they get here?”

“We gather everyone we can save and run.” I swallowed hard, keeping my eyes on the lights growing ever closer.

This is going to be a massacre.

Turning on my heels, I quickly made my way to a man cleaning a few medical supplies. Taking a few from the tray, I began copying his actions. No one spoke. Only the approaching bangs and distant shouts broke the silence. We continued to prepare ourselves for the onslaught- gathering clean cloth, getting clean water, assembling medicine, and on and on. It felt like only seconds were going by. Anxiety ate away at me as every muscle in my body felt like ants were crawling in them. Just as I felt like breathing wasn’t so much of a chore, a blaring horn reverberated. Everyone froze. Time stood still as all eyes watched the main road.

“They’re coming!” a woman amongst us shouted, her voice shaking in terror.

No one responded. No one even looked at her. All eyes zeroed in on the flash of light just on the opposite end of town. The vibration of thousands of boots pounding, gunfire blasting, swords clashing against each other, and screams were deafening. A low ringing began in my ears.

I can’t breathe…

With one final gunshot, dozens of our soldiers began to pour in from every direction. Nearly all of them were covered head to toe in blood. Some stopped, turning around to create a defensive line while others hobbled desperately towards us- half of them with a limp body slung over their shoulders dripping with crimson liquid.

Oh no...

“Help the injured!” Charlotte ordered breaking all of us out of our stupor. Before we could comply, the soldiers ran past us. They scurried by without so much as a glance as they made their way through the escape path towards Fallbell.

Why are they leaving?

"Forget the medical tent- we need to evacuate now!" a member of the guard shouted as he stopped in front of Charlotte. Said woman frowned as she motioned to the men still running past us.

"They need immediate medical attention to survive the journey to-"

"If we don't leave now then all of us will die!" The man shouted back glaring down at her now shocked expression. "There are too many of them and we can't hold them for much longer! Take only what you absolutely need and *run*!" The moment the words left his lips, a building directly across from us exploded. The blast knocked all of us to the ground. Debris and dust polluted the air making it nearly impossible to breathe. The incessant ringing in my ears reached a fever pitch, causing a nauseating ache to pierce my skull.

What was that?

Staggering to my feet, I glanced around only to see Charlotte dragging one of the women from underneath a table that collapsed on top of her. Dirt covered her face and scratches littered her visible skin. Her wide frantic eyes scanned her surroundings in a panic. Seeing the man, I helped clean supplies with early come to her aid, I turned my attention towards the rubble that once was a house. From the pile of bricks and wood, a swarm of soldiers clothed in black with red trims invaded, their weapons ready to strike down anyone that dared to cross their path.

How are there still so many of them left?

"Jayde Henryk!" My head snapped up just in time to see a burly man making his way towards me, his unsettlingly milky white eyes held no emotion. A crooked grin was frozen on his face and a massive axe dripping in blood in his hands. "Looks like my lucky day! I get to kill you for Lord Hawk!" without warning, the man swung his axe at my head with a speed I thought was impossible for a weapon that size.

Hitting the dirt, I rolled away from him as he slashed down at me. Frantically looking across the ground for any form of weapon, my eyes locked on a large knife. Lunging for it just as he sliced at me, I gripped it tightly in my hand. Getting to my feet, I squared off against him. Keeping my stance low, I barely kept the panic that filled me at bay. The man's grin only widened.

"What do you think you're going to do with that, little girl?" I didn't dare respond- I don't trust my voice not to show the overwhelming fear I feel. Instead, I tightened my grip on the knife holding it close to my body.

I'm not going down!

He laughed as he swung his axe horizontally. Using speed I didn't know I possessed, I side stepped it. Aiming for his face and squeezing my eyes shut, I slashed out with as much power as I could muster.

The feeling of thick, sticky liquid splashing on my skin and clothing followed by a cry of agony told me that I hit my mark. Opening my eyes, my jaw dropped in horror at the sight of the man on his knees screaming and holding his face. Blood oozed from between his fingers as his right hand grip his axe tightly, turning his knuckles white. Profanities and insults spewed from his lips, but the bile rising into my throat barely made me aware of his words.

What do I do now?

"Jayde!" my head snapped up in time to see Ginger running towards us, a sword in her right hand covered in blood.

The man tried to stand, but Ginger was much faster. Launching herself into the air, she used her momentum to kick him into the dirt. Before he could do anything else, she plunged her sword through his back and into his heart. Roughly yanking it out, the man heaved for only a second before his body went completely still.

Panting, Ginger quickly moved towards me, her eyes examining me for injuries. She paused when she saw the knife in my hand before her eyes glanced back down at the body. Understanding shined in her eyes, as a gentle look came over her bloodied face.

Reaching out, she took my left hand in hers giving it a tight squeeze. My brain wouldn't do anything more than look at her while slowly processing the words that left her lips.

"We need to get out of here!" she shouted over the chaos happening around us. "There are more of them than we thought. We can't hold them back any longer!" I dumbly nod lowering my head to stare at the ground muddied with blood and dirt. In the next second, Ginger released my hand bringing both of her hands up to cup my face raising my head to look her in the eye. "Jayde, I need you to help evacuate the injured. We need as many people as we can to help keep Hawk's men off of your trail, alright?" Nodding once more, she smiled at me letting her hands slip from my face. "Good. I'm counting on you." With one last encouraging smile, she twirled on her heels and sprinted back into the fray, dodging blows and dealing fatal attacks as she went.

Taking one last shaky breath, I scanned the area for someone who needed help when my eyes spotted a woman trying to crawl.

Tears streamed down her cheeks as her fingers dug into the ground. Her right leg left behind a trail of crimson as it lagged behind her limply. With adrenaline coursing through my veins, I ran to her. She looked at me with wide eyes as I slung her arm over my shoulders. Hoisting her up as much as I could, I half dragged her towards the escape route.

"Y-you shouldn't be here- why are you still here?" She shouted at me, her voice filled with pain.

"Well, we're leaving now."

"I wouldn't say so, Jayde Henryk."

Do I have a literal *target on me?! How do they keep finding me in all this chaos?!*

Turning, a brawny man stood before us. Six gold medals hung from the lapel of his uniform. An expensive looking belt hung from his waist holding two cutlasses and two pistols. Just like the guy from before, a fog covered his emotionless eyes, a smirk snaking onto his lips.

He must be a general. Lucky him.

"Lord Hawk has been searching for you."

"It doesn't seem like I'm that hard to find." I shot back, the terror I feel being replaced with frustration.

Why do innocent people keep dying because of me?!

"No, it doesn't." He mused, pulling out one of his pistols from his waistband. "But in the end, it is inevitable that *he* will be victorious." My body tensed. I readied to push the woman out of the way.

His finger flexed, but a sword came flying from behind me logging itself deep into his throat. The man spluttered for a few seconds, before he fell backwards into the dirt. Twirling, I was barely able to see Ginger whirl in time to disarm a soldier, take their sword and continue to fight.

"What are you still doing here, stray? This ain't a place for you?" I've never been more relieved to hear that insulting tone of voice in my life.

"Singer." I breathed as the light around him died down.

He paused- more than likely noticing the gallon of blood coating my body- before he turned his eyes towards the battle. Without a word, he brought his hands in front of his face forming a diamond. A ball of grey mist formed in the middle before he softly blew into it. Immediately, the mist spread out, rapidly engulfing the area in under a second. Just as quickly as it came, it dissipated.

Hawk's men were left on the ground with blood pooling in their mouths while our side were left in a confused stupor. Not wasting a second, our men began to bolt towards the escape route. I could feel the ground vibrate as more of Hawk's soldiers closed in.

"Get moving!" Singer ordered. Pulling the woman from me, Singer hoisted her across his shoulders in one fluid tug, his sword appearing in his right hand. "Now!" Not needing to be told twice, I sprinted after him.

We ran until the dense wilderness surrounded us. Behind us, at least a hundred of Hawk's men were giving chase- the cries of agony told me that without having to look. Singer expertly led the way around the trees and over the foliage that disguised the traps beneath them.

Please don't let them catch up to us!

"Jayde, Singer!"

Cadian!

Glancing over my shoulder, Ginger and Cadian sprinted towards us until they ran with us.

"I'm so happy to see you two alive!" I shouted, tears pricking the back of my eyes.

This isn't the time to cry!

"Just a few scratches and bruises- nothing a little rest can't heal." Cadian responded, but I didn't miss the sideways glance he shot Ginger.

Why does he look so worried?

Analyzing her form from the corner of my eye, I noticed the fresh flow of blood flowing down the right side of her stomach.

She's hurt!

I opened my mouth to say something, but the soft smile Ginger shot me silenced me. It screamed for me to stay silent and that she will be fine.

I hope she's right.

I shook my head, ridding myself of the thought.

We ran for another five minutes when the adrenaline that kept me going dissipated. My body felt sluggish as the pain that has been blocked from my consciousness flooded me in a tidal wave. Panting heavily, I pushed myself to keep up with the group's fast pace, but my legs began to shake from exhaustion.

No- I have to keep going! I can't stop!

A scream ripped through my throat as a body crashed into me, sending us both tumbling to the ground. The moment we stopped rolling, my attacker twisted until they were on top of me, using all of their weight to pin me down. My visions tunneled on the woman, her eyes holding the fogginess all of Hawk's soldiers have.

"Die, Jayde Henryk!" My eyes widened as she raised a knife over her head. Before she could plunge it into my heart, a shadow shoved her to the side. I scrambled away as the figure wrestled with the woman. Singer, Ginger, and Cadian moved in front of me, forming a protective line. Within a couple of seconds, the figure disarmed the woman, jamming the knife into the woman's neck. The figure paused for a second before standing and turning towards us.

"Dove!" She frowned at me before her head snapped in the direction of Redmage. Turning back to me, she took long strides until she was directly in front of me.

"We need to move. Now." Before I could even respond, Dove had my hand in her grasps pulling me behind her as we all sprinted down the path again.

"How much longer do we have until we reach Fallbell?" I shouted to Dove. She didn't answer me as we continued to run.

"Don't worry, Jayde. We'll be there-" a deafening bang and the sound of a body hitting the floor left me frozen in my steps.

No-

"Ginger!" Snatching my hand from Dove, I whirled around to see the red-haired woman face down in the dirt. A hole in the middle of her back poured blood. "No!" I ran to her not even paying attention to the others as they took out the soldiers that caught up to us. Pressing my hands to the wound, tears flooded my face. "You're going to be okay- you're going to be okay."

"Jayde..." my head snapped up. Ginger looked at me through half lidded eyes. A gentle smile lay on her lips as her breath came in shallow huffs.

"Ginger! I can't-" Her smile only widened as she took my hand in hers giving it a weak squeeze.

"Jayde... remember your promise... to care for Karlie for me."

"I promise." I sobbed holding her hand tighter in mine.

"Good... good..." her hand went limp in mine, one last breath passed through her lips.

My heart squeezed as I felt her pulse beginning to weaken.

"No, no- you're not dying!" I shouted, scalding tears streaming down my cheeks.

Ripping a strip of cloth from the bottom of my shirt, I wrapped it around her wound, tying it securely in place. Hoisting her onto my back, I took a second to make sure she wouldn't fall. Glancing at the others, I felt my heart stop.

Dove refused to look at me, tears falling from her eyes.

Cadian's face was filled with grief before he had to avert his gaze. Singer held an expression that I'd never seen before. Is that... sympathy?

No- no, no, no- she's still alive!

She's still warm- she's not cold! I can feel her heart beating against my back. If she were dead, that wouldn't happen. All I have to do is get her to Charlotte. As long as I do that, then she'll live!

Turning away from them, I took off down the path as fast as I could. Behind me, I heard three sets of feet keeping pace. The darkening sky and the stench of decay at our backs.

***

By the time night fell nearly an hour later, we made it to Fallbell. Thanks to the faye, Hawk's army won't be able to pursue us. There's a plethora of traps and illusions set up that won't let up until tomorrow. So, at least for tonight, we can gather ourselves and rest without worry.

Ginger will be ok by then.

Quickly locating the medical tent, I sprinted straight towards it. My legs ached and my back was screaming in pain, but I kept moving.

I won't let Hawk take Ginger from Karlie! I won't let him ruin another family!

Bursting through the tents flaps, the medics inside only took a moment to acknowledge me before they jumped into action.

Charlotte was in front of me in a flash along with two males taking Ginger off of my back. Rushing her over to a red stained cot, they laid her down gently. Charlotte gingerly untied the cloth from her wound. As her eyes assessed the damage, a sorrowful glint passed through her eyes. She checked Ginger's pulse before her shoulders slumped.

What is she doing?

"Why aren't you doing anything - why aren't you helping her?" I screamed, tears coming down my face. Charlotte slowly turned towards me, giving me a grim look.

"There's nothing we can do for her." My breath hitched as my knees gave out.

No- no- no-no-no!

"She's still alive! I felt her-" my breath hitched, my heart twisting painfully. Charlotte only spared me one more mournful glance before rushing to another patient. I barely registered the woman Singer was carrying being placed on a cot opposite of Ginger.

Stumbling forward, I stopped next to Ginger.

The world seemed to stop as I looked over her ashen face, a peaceful smile on her blue lips. My own breath sounds unbelievably loud in my ears.

She's gone... for what? Why? What did she do to deserve this?

Vaguely, I felt someone come behind me. They rubbed my back while guiding me away from Ginger and out of the tent. The last thing I saw before the flaps closed was a woman covering Ginger's body with a white sheet.

Stumbling, I turned around to gaze around the camp. Women, children, the elderly, and the surviving combatants were everywhere.

None of them were joyous- none of them showed relief at surviving. *All* of them looked like they had been dragged through hell. *All* of them held a shadow of death over their heads as they watched the lifeless bodies of their comrades be carried to the back of the camp to be buried. Most of the people cried out in excruciating pain for their lost loved ones while the others tried their best to comfort them. *I can't- I can't do this! I can't- I can't-*

Before I knew it, I was looking in the direction of Redmage. Smoke rose into the sky as a red and orange glow emitted. Are they burning the town or are the bodies?

How many bodies did we have to leave behind?

"There you are, stray." My eyes drifted down until they landed on Singer's approaching figure. The moment our eyes connected, a frown settled on his lips stopping him in his tracks. "Go to bed, stray. We're going to be up bright and early tomorrow." I nodded numbly, dropping my gaze to my feet.

My legs hurt so much before but I can't feel them anymore...

His frown deepened as he placed a hand on my shoulder. With a soft push, he guided me towards one of the four large tents on the other side of camp. As we walked, we passed the rest of our army- the rest of the survivors. There were three bon fires set up in the middle of camp. Those who surrounded them sat in silence. It wasn't comfortable, peaceful, or even somber. It was *grueling.*

The elderly held wailing children while silent tears cascaded down their sunken cheeks. Fighters hung their heads; stained bandages wrapped around their wounds. Others lay curled in tight balls, screaming in anguish. All of those cries echoed endlessly in my head that I barely realized we were standing in front of a tent.

Moving the flaps to the side, Singer nudged me inside. As the flaps slid closed, the cries silenced. He led me to one of the empty cots in the far back corner. The others either had belongings on top or someone already sleeping on it. Motioning for me to lay down, I did. Settling on my side, I hugged my knees to my chest, allowing the tears to freely flow down my cheeks. Singer sat on the ground beside me, resting his back against the side of my cot.

"Singer," the sound of my voice being so hollow and lifeless shocked me, "is this how every battle is going to be?" he was silent for a long time before he let out a soft sigh.

"I don't know about war," he started, his tone gentle, "but battles are always ugly. They're dirty, cruel, and grueling. People are bound to die, and for every life lost, there're a hundred more affected. But," he turned his head to look me in the eye. His shined with a tenderness I didn't know he was capable of. "I've never regretted fighting, nor have I ever met anyone that has." Nodding silently, I let out a shaky breath. "Go to sleep. I'll keep watch." Singer finally said, facing forward. Bending one of his knees, he rested his arm on top of it. I watched him for a second longer before the corners of my lips rose the slightest.

"Thank you, Singer." I whispered as I closed my eyes. My consciousness quickly began to slip away, but I heard the last words Singer whispered before a dreamless sleep took hold of me.

"Good night... Jayde."

XIII

Before the sun rose above the horizon, we were marching to Bellhall. We packed the camp in such a rush that we left most of the supplies behind. Only the medical and two of the sleeping tents were brought. The others were left behind- burned so they couldn't be used by Hawk's army. Turning my head slightly, a lump formed in my throat as my tired eyes burned from unshed tears.

The throng of people carrying nothing bigger than a sack over their shoulders met my gaze. Children carried what little they could, but the unmistakable signs of a sleepless night covered their faces. One of the worst amongst them was Karlie. She walked next to one of the older nomad women who, apparently, is her great aunt. Both of them held pronounced dark circles under their eyes, their heads facing the ground. A blanket of dread covered us as we continued to move on - never stopping for fear our enemy would catch up to us.

How are we supposed to survive for another day like this?

Taking a deep breath, I faced forward, my shoulders slumping. Maybe, when this is all over - and if I'm still alive - I'll come back and visit the graves. After all, they died because of me - *because of the power of a jewel coveted by a mad man.*

"What are you moping about, stray?" Singer admonished, appearing beside me. I didn't respond. How could I when there's nothing lighthearted or easygoing to say?

Because I'm alive, more and more people are going to die... what is there to joke about?

Apparently, Singer could read the look on my face because he let out a soft hum before turning his gaze straight.

"Save your mourning for the dead until after the war is over." *What did he just say?*

"Just because I care about the deaths of hundreds of innocent people and you don't doesn't give you the right to-"

"I think the idea," Cadian's voice rang, cutting me off, "wasn't supposed to be so cruel." Shooting Singer a look above my head, Cadian gave him a frown before turning his soft gaze back down to me. "Though he could have phrased it better."

"Since you seem to be such an expert in the art of interpreting insufferable jerks, then please, explain what he was trying to say." I shot back, quickening my pace. Cadian was silent for a few seconds before raising his gaze to the sky.

"Thinking about those who died at a time like this will only end up distracting you, thus, getting you killed. What do you think will happen to the rest of us if you die?"

You all die.

"That will only make all of the lives that were lost yesterday be in vain- and that's a terrible way to repay their sacrifice." My heart sunk as my eyes closed.

He's right.

Slowing my pace, a sigh left my lips as an image of Karlie came to the forefront of my mind.

The scene from this morning is something I never want to experience again. It was like looking back into the past when I first found out I had lost my family, but someone had to tell her. Someone had to explain to her why her precious auntie didn't return to her last night. Someone had to explain to her why her beloved auntie is *never* going to come back. Someone had to... and since it's my fault, who better to take on that burden?

At first, everything seemed to go well. Karlie looked as if she understood when I told her what happened to Ginger while we were escaping.

I was wrong.

She immediately demanded that she be allowed to visit her in the medical tent. However, when I explained that she wasn't there- that she didn't survive- she broke down. She didn't just cry, she collapsed in *agony.*

She shouldn't have to experience loss like this at her age- she's just a child!

Then again, no one should have to deal with this kind of pain - no one.

"I understand." I finally whispered.

A suffocating silence followed with only the sounds of our feet smashing in the dirt breaking it. A few seconds later, Singer sniffed loudly, holding his head high and his back straight.

"Get a move on before the group leaves you, stray." He proclaimed walking faster.

Is he being serious right now?

"But," he started cutting off my rampage before it could even start, "if you're too exhausted from putting up a... *passable* effort yesterday, then I guess I can carry you- but only this *once*!"

... *Did I hear him right?*

"Wha- what?" Blinking twice, I shook my head, a frown on my face. "Do... do you really think I did anything noteworthy?" He grunted in response scratching the shell of his elongated ear.

"Let's not get carried away. Your efforts were pitiful at best, but I guess you could've done *much* worse. For you, that deserves some level of acknowledgement. Besides," he turned slightly, his face blank besides a nondescript glint in his eyes.

Is that pride?

"You didn't abandon a friend when most people would've."

Tears wield up in my eyes, a stupid grin forming on my face.

"Thank you... Singer." Shock flashed across his features before he scoffed snapping forward once more.

"Are you going to accept my offer? I'm not going to keep it open forever you know." Inwardly, I laughed.

Without wasting another moment, I stepped closer to him, putting my hands on his shoulders. On cue, he bent down allowing me to climb onto his back. When I was secure, he stood up straight continuing on the path after Cadian who moved ahead of us, a knowing smile on his face.

Who knew Singer could be so... comforting. First last night and now this?

"Just to reiterate in case you forgot in the last twenty seconds," *Here we go.*

"*Never* mention this again." My smile widened as I held on to him tighter.

"I wouldn't dream of it, you insufferable jerk."

***

About an hour and a half later we made it to Bellhall. Unlike in Redmage, the townspeople haven't been evacuated. Almost everyone that can hold a weapon is geared for battle. Everyone else is gathered in the very back of town on the border to the forest where a medical tent is already set up. Besides, where are they supposed to go? The closest town is nearly an hour walk south west from where we came from and, even then, Hawk's men are more than likely preparing to trap us against the forest and their guns. What other choice do we have but to stand and fight?

Run into the forest and hope the faye got the message not to kill us?

"Alright, we made it- now get off me, stray." Singer mumbled. I half expected him to drop me. When he crouched with an expectant look on his face, my jaw nearly dropped in shock. Sliding off his back, I shot him a questioning side eye.

"What's gotten into you?" The look he sent me over his shoulder was much softer than anything I'd seen from him. I guess he noticed, because he quickly turned away, making a dramatic show of stretching his back.

"I don't know what you're talking about, stray." I watched him for a second longer before a small grin stretched my lips.

"Don't tell me- you really *do* like me?" He whirled towards me with an offended scowl, but the dust of pink on his cheeks showed the truth. Singer opened his mouth to speak, but a distinct and mournfully familiar horn cut him off.

"They've caught up to us!"

"They're attacking the rear!"

Not again!

Dove ran past us, her lance in hand.

"All infantry men, ready on me!" She ordered as she bolted pass. Some of the men and a few of the women immediately followed, giving their loved ones a goodbye.

There's no way he could've caught up to us so quickly!

"Stay back with the medics, stray." I didn't even get a chance to respond to him as the sounds of battle reached my ears.

They're almost here!

"Go!" Singer shouted, giving me a rough shove to the side, knocking me to the ground. A second later, an arrow whizzed through the air where my head once was. Just as he summoned his sword in a flash of white light, I scrambled to my feet, sprinting off towards the other side of the village.

I made it half way there when a scream of pain stopped me in my tracks. Whirling around, I braced myself. A soldier ripped a bloody spear from the back of an elderly man. The man fell to the ground in a lifeless heap, blood pouring from his lips. The soldier made eye contact with me, a crooked grin forming on his face. Before he could do anything else, Cadian jumped from the roof of a building- a dagger in his hands- and landed on the man's back, knocking both of them to the ground. They wrestled for a second before Cadian landed the fatal blow. Panting, he rose to his feet, turning his steely eyes to me.

"Get to the medics, now, Jayde."

I can't breathe…

My body went numb as the bedlam crashed down on my consciousness all at once. The gun shots - the arrows - the knives - the spears piercing through bodies- the swords slicing flesh - *the corpses covering the ground.*

My heart skipped a beat, a painful knot forming in my chest, bile rising in my throat.

All because of me- everyone is dying because of me!

"Why..." Cadian looked taken aback, but shook his head taking a step towards me.

"Jayde-"

"Why won't he just kill me already!" I screamed. Several soldiers turned towards me. They looked stunned at my outburst, but once they realized who I was, disgusting smiles of blood lust covered their faces.

"Kill the Henryk!"

"Kill the last survivor!" With that, all of them lunged at me.

Let them try!

I glared at every single one of them as they came at me.

They call me the last survivor for a reason!

I could see Cadian yelling at me from the corner of my eye as he tried to get to me, but he was too far away, and the soldiers were closing in too fast. Just as they came within striking distance, a black mass dropped from the sky crushing one under it. The rest halted, the mist coating their eyes subsided only for a moment as fear shined through. In a flash of silver, the remaining ones lay dead before me. With the sound of rustling feathers, my eyes widened as my savior slowly turned, his yellow eyes narrowed.

"What have I told you about being reckless?"

"Favian?" I took a step away, alarm bells ringing in my head.

The look on his face was anything but friendly.

"Don't be foolish again." In the next breath, a rumble vibrated the ground growing more and more apparent. Not even a second later, an army of a thousand Hobbes and goblins flooded into the area, their crude weapons at the ready and a battle cry of jumbled babble in their wake. Hawk's men faltered as their unbridled blood lust was replaced with horror.

Just like that the tide of the battle turned in our favor. Before their arrival, we were miserably outnumbered and outgunned, but now, we stand a chance of winning.

Hawk's men were being taken out left and right. A nearby hobbe launched itself at a soldier. Scaling their back with its thin arms, it wrapped its bony legs around their neck and bit their face. The hobbe's wide jaws clamped down across the soldier's face. Their tiny, sharp teeth shredded the skin as the soldier screamed and tried to rip the little monster off. Within seconds, the hobbe snapped his neck with its powerful jaws. The soldier went limp, crumbling to the ground.

Other hobbes worked in pairs to attack. I saw one hobbe use a broken branch to bash a soldier's knee. A loud snap followed by screams of pain blended into the array of chaos. The soldier collapsed to the ground, his leg jutting out to his side at a right angle. His cries were quickly silenced by a second hobbe smashing his head with a heavily rusted hammer. They screeched at the sky in excitement before catapulting at another soldier.

Even the goblins were a lethal force. Wielding rusted, broken swords and axes, they barreled through the enemy. A trail of limbs lay in their wake as they sliced and slashed. The sight was nearly enough to convince me we had a chance to win this- to survive.

That is, until the soldiers started fighting back.

Maybe it was the power of the jewel, but the initial surprise that broke through the mind control wore off. As if something flipped, our enemy mercilessly retaliated. The hobbes that once were tearing them apart were quickly being stomped and hacked to death. Goblins were cleared in half, but it didn't mean all hope were lost. The nomads worked to protect the dark faye. Parrying swords and blocking arrows before they could strike. Even the hobbes and goblins threw themselves into helping the nomads. Tripping soldiers to be easier targets and launching themselves at enemies that were about to kill one of our own. Seeing Hobbes, goblins, and nomads fighting side by side - it's almost laughable.

Even though he was the only one, Favian was a terrifying sight. Diving at breakneck speeds, he cut through lines of men before impaling the last. Taking their bodies high into the sky, he threw them back into the mass like a cannon ball. As their body collided, groups of soldiers would fall leaving them open for the ground forces to kill.

He only spared a second before doing it again.

The monarchs don't disappoint, do they?

Before I could even register what happened, I found myself on the ground, a throbbing pain in my chest.

"I've finally found you." My blood ran cold as my lungs began to close.

Hawk…

Looking up at him, all I could see was the monster that's haunted me ever since that fateful night.

Since the last time I saw him, Hawk turned from a healthy young man probably in his late twenties to a grotesque beast. His skin is sickly pale, a stark contrast to the light tan he once had. His eyes are wide and glazed over with a deep rooted madness that shone from the prominent dark circles under his eyes. The once thick mane of hair that sat on top of his head thinned out considerably. Instead of the muscled, lean figure he once sported, he thinned out to the point that some of his bones are easily seen.

That's why they say the jewel is cursed.

"You have no idea how long I've waited for this!" A smirk stretched his chapped lips, his bony fingers slowly pulled out the sword on his belt with practiced ease. "It's just like I've always imagined!" With that said, he took a step closer, raising his sword.

Do something, Jayde!

From the corner of my eye, I spotted a fallen shield. Crawling towards it, I snatched it from the ground and held it up in front of me, but Hawk easily kicked it out of my grasp. Before I could do anything else, he pressed his foot on my stomach pinning me to the ground.

No! I won't die like this!

Flailing my arms and legs, I tried my hardest to knock him off- or at least get his heavy foot off of me! In the end, my efforts only made him laugh in dry amusement.

"Oh Jayde, always fighting until the bloody end. If things were different, I might have let you live- if only to experience the thrill of hunting you down." With one more bellowing laugh, he unsheathed the sword at his waist at a tauntingly slow pace. I struggled harder, tears filling my eyes. "Goodbye. Tell your parents I said hello."

No!

"Jayde!" Cadian shouted, sprinting towards us. In a swift motion, he took out three soldiers that tried to block his path. Without even glancing behind him, Hawk whipped out the pistol on his waist, aimed, and fired. Clutching his right side, Cadian hit the ground three feet away.

"No!" Cadian's body twitched as he coughed up blood.

"No one will save you from me!" Hawk's demented eyes practically bulged as he pulled back his arm. Before he could stab me, a pained cry left his lips. He stumbled back holding his bloodied calf, removing his foot from on top of me. Quickly scrambling away, I looked to the side to see Cadian. He held his blood-stained dagger in his hands, pain shining in his eyes as he looked at me.

"Run... Jayde." Letting out one final breath, his head hit the dirt, his body going limp.

"Cadian!"

"You insolent little wretch!" Hawk screeched, taking his uninjured foot and kicking Cadian's body roughly.

"Stop it!" I screamed, the tears I've been holding back finally cascading down my face. His wild eyes turned on me.

"I will have more power! I *need* more power!" Dejavu hit me like a ton of bricks as he aimed his gun at me.

How did this end the last time?

His finger flexed to pull the trigger, but a blinding white light appeared between us. Squeezing my eyes shut, I covered my face. Seconds later, the light died down, revealing a sight that left my heart in my throat, my stomach in an agonizing knot, and my lungs constricted.

"A...Aric..." I whispered. The little boy I thought- *hoped-* would one day return stood between me and Hawk, his arms stretched out wide in a protective stance.

"Leave Jay alone!" He screamed, shocking me to my core.

He's really here!

Before Hawk could respond, the ground gave a violent shake, a black fog rose encasing the area. I felt a tiny pinch before it dissipated. When it vanished, Hawk's army was gone. Only our side was present in the middle of a clearing surrounded by trees.

We're in the forest? But how?

"The fairy king must have activated his emergency plan. I guess things went too far south for his liking." Favian explained, fluttering down from the sky, his arms folded across his chest.

So that's why.

With that solved, my mind solely focused on the boy before me. Slowly, he turned to me, a wicked smile on his face. A gasp left my lips as my eyes fully took in his features. His ears were elongated like Singer's and his bright amber eyes held the faintest specks of blue in their depths. Other than that, he looked just as I remembered. A head of curly, black hair that brushed the top of his eyebrows. His round, chubby cheeks framed his face. The bridge of his nose held the slightest hint of freckles breaking up his smooth brown skin- the same shade as mine. The smile on his face only widened at my roaming eyes.

"I've missed you, Jay." He softly spoke, his eyes softening.

He's here- he's really here!

A choked sob left my throat catching him off guard. As he opened his mouth, I threw my arms around him, squeezing him as tightly as I possibly could.

"Ricky!" He's alive- he's alive-

He's alive!

No one said anything as I cried, leaving my heart and soul my sleeve.

My baby brother is back!

XIV

"How much longer?" Aric pouted as he looked up at me. I smiled, giving his hand a squeeze.

"We're almost there." I whispered. Understanding flashed through his eyes as he turned his attention forward once more.

Maybe I should carry him? He did just come back. Isn't this too much on his body?

We've been trudging through the forest for the better part of an hour. Everyone is more than exhausted and some need medical attention as soon as possible. Though this battle wasn't nearly as bad as yesterday's, it still left a scar on everyone.

At least none of the children had to witness it. I don't know what I would do if Aric or Karlie saw what happened back there.

"We've made it!" A man shouted from the front. Aric let out a sigh of relief. Quickening his pace, he dragged me behind him as he excitedly rushed forward.

"Come on Jay!" The excitement in his voice brightened my sour mood if only by a little.

Watching him makes it easy to forget about reality for a moment.

Within a minute, we entered a small clearing filled with towering tents surrounding a large fire pit. White and purple pixies fluttered around the vicinity, lighting the outer rim of camp.

Not too long ago, Aric was one of them.

Just the thought of Aric leaving me again was enough to make my heart ache.

I won't let that happen again.

"Jay, are you okay?" Looking down at him, a smile touched my lips.

"I'm fine, Ricky." Tugging his arm gently, I pulled him towards me. Holding him close, I guided us further into the camp.

A look of confusion passed across his adorable face, but he didn't say anything. Instead, his gaze wandered around to watch the pixies. Awe covered his features as he watched them float, shining their brilliant colors before drifting away. He looked as if he wanted to say something but refrained.

What does he want to say? Don't tell… does he remember his past?

In a flash, Dove's story hit me. Of how she remembered her family. How they lived.

How they died.

I swallowed hard, my heart clenching painfully.

Please- I'd rather he forgets me than remember that!

Shutting my eyes briefly, I forced the thoughts from my mind.

Why get myself worked up? Maybe, just maybe, he won't remember anything.

Squeezing Aric a little tighter, we kept walking. We moved towards the bonfire and settled down beside it. Placing Aric in my lap, I hugged him to me, rocking us back and forth gently. Closing my eyes, the faces of all our comrades - living and dead - flashed across my consciousness.

How can I make sure that all of them survive? I don't think I can live through burying another friend.

"Jayde Henryk?" Opening my eyes, I titled my head up to see a woman standing before me. Her dark pink eyes were sharp, but held a soft edge. Her dark blue hair was tied in a high ponytail showing off her elongated ears. Diamond shaped emerald earrings that swayed every time she moved her head adorned them.

"What is it?"

"The monarchs require your presence. Your companions-

Dove and Singer- are already heading there."

"I *was* until I remembered this stray would get lost in an open field if you left her alone." Singer grumbled as he approached us. I raised a brow at him before looking back over to the woman.

"I won't leave my brother alone." Singer grunted, making an exasperated gesture around the camp.

"Where else is he supposed to go? Daycare?" With an exaggerated sigh, Singer closed the distance between us.

Reaching down, he gripped the back of Aric's shirt and, with one fluid motion, swung Aric over his shoulder, keeping a firm grasp of his shirt. Without another word, he began walking away towards the largest tent that practically glowed like a beacon with the hundreds of pixies that surrounded it.

"S-Singer-"

"Are you coming or not, stray?"

"Singer!" I yelled running after him. "Be gentle with him! He just came back- we don't know how fragile he is!"

"Calm down! The brat will be fine as long as he doesn't use too much magic. Something like this won't affect him." With that said, Singer picked up his pace.

Well, why didn't he just say that to begin with?

"Just...just be careful. Fairy or not- he's still just a kid."

"Yeah, sure, whatever you say." Singer nonchalantly said, swatting aside the flaps to the tent.

We both stepped inside to see hundreds of pixies floating in the air lighting up the room in a magical aura. Sitting directly across from us are Bellatrix, Alastar, and Elah. All three of them sat on large thrones decorated in vines and leaves, a large oval table separated Bellatrix from Alastar and Elah. On the table lay a large map of the world with a few stone figurines strategically placed on top.

Are they preparing for the next battle?

Singer grunted, stepping further into the room until he stood directly in front of the table. He looked between all of the monarchs before swinging Aric in front of him. Unceremoniously, he plopped him on the ground. Aric looked dazed before he gazed up at Singer with a small frown.

He did not *just dump him on the floor like that!*

Slowly, Singer turned his head until he faced me, an unmistakable smirk on his face.

"Is this better, stray?"

That little-

I shook my head. No, I can always punish him for this later. Rushing over to Aric's side, I knelt, taking his smaller hands into my own.

"Are you alright?" he glanced at me before turning his attention back to Singer, a wide grin on his face.

"That was fun! Can we do that again?"

Resisting the urge to smack my forehead, I ignored Singer's mocking laughter opting to help Aric to his feet.

"I don't think that's going to happen." I mumbled straightening out his ruffled clothing. Confusion covered his chubby features before understanding shined in his eyes.

"You don't have to worry about me, Jay- I'm tough!" I couldn't stop the smile that stretched across my lips.

"Of course you are." Holding out my hand to him, he happily took it. With one last smile to him and a glare to Singer, I turned to face the monarchs already anticipating their amused faces from our little charade.

Well, at least from Bellatrix and Alastar at least.

As I thought, Bellatrix watched us with mirth sparkling in her eyes while Alastar barely held back his laughter. Elah, on the other hand, looked far from entertained. Her face showed she was on the verge of killing us for wasting her precious time.

Well, she can get over it.

"It's good to see you all alive and well." Bellatrix started, nodding her head towards Singer and me.

"Well, it's not like I was ever in any *real* danger, but your concern is flattering." Singer smugly responded. Bellatrix giggled as I elbowed him harshly on his side.

Seriously, can he show respect to anybody?

"As for you, my new little fairy." A light blush dusted across

Aric's cheeks as he shifted his weight from side to side. "I'm glad to see you finally decided to wake up." The red on his cheeks deepened as he shot his head up to look her in the eye.

"I had to protect Jay!" my jaw went slack in shock as I looked down at him.

What?

His eyes widened as he quickly looked away.

So he came back just to save me from Hawk?

A smile stretched across my lips, my eyes softening as the blush on his face deepened.

You don't have to protect me anymore, Ricky. From now on, I'll protect you.

"Don't stare at me like that, Jay." He mumbled, shifting uncomfortably and twiddling with his fingers. I inwardly laughed, giving his hand a squeeze.

Still as cute as always.

"Not that this isn't sweet and all that mushy stuff," Singer started, taking a step forward to stand beside me, "why don't we focus on something more important? Like- I don't know- the army of brainwashed humans with lots of guns and cannons?"

Way to ruin a moment.

A frown settled on my lips.

"No matter how much it pains me to admit, he's right." My grip tightened around Aric's hand, "We need a plan to take care of Hawk. He's already taken too much from everyone- and I'm not willing to let him continue." From the corner of my eye, Ricky looked up at me, his eyes glazed over with sadness.

"I'll be fine, Jay. I promise." Blinking slowly, I let out an inaudible breath. He doesn't understand how bad everything was after *that* night.

"Don't worry about the boy." Turning my gaze to Alastar, a small smirk filled with barely contained mischief stared back at me. "You forget that our goal is to prevent Hawk from killing every one of the Henryk bloodline. Aric is a Henryk and, therefore, under our protection- and I don't accept failure." The smirk on his face grew as hope filled me.

When the king of the most powerful army in the world tells you that you're going to be fine, you tend to believe him. Anyone who can command the obedience of hobbes and goblins is someone not to be trifled with.

I can only imagine what the army he's bringing this time will look like.

"I hope that's so," everyone turned to the entrance as Dove entered. Her lance in her hands, a small scratch leaking red violet sat on the hollow of her cheek. "Because Hawk is bringing even more soldiers than before."

"How is that possible?" I whispered, my eyes going wide as my heart pounded in my chest.

How- where did they come from?

"What have you learned from your reconnaissance?" Bellatrix smoothly asked, gesturing Dove to come closer.

"Hawk only sent half of his army for the initial assault. The other half was still in Clearapal recruiting more people and gathering supplies to bring for a final battle."

"So, that means his entire army is here now?" Dove shifted her eyes to Singer, her lips in a grim line.

"Yes."

"How many?"

"Well over eight thousand."

"Wow, you seriously missed the mark on this one, amateur. How many did you say there was to begin with?" Ignoring him, Dove turned back to Bellatrix.

"What do you wish for your people to do?" Bellatrix looked thoughtful for a moment before leaning back, crossing her arms under her chest.

"What do you suggest, darling?"

"I suggest we split into three groups. The first squadron will meet the enemy along the border of the forest. The second will be their back-up or the next line of defense for when the enemy breaks through the initial line. What's left of the enemy will face the final line-"

"Now why does this give me a horrible case of deja-vu?" Singer interrupted, his face uncharacteristically blank. Dove wasn't perturbed one bit.

"That's because we used the same strategy during the first attack."

"And was I the only one to see how well that turned out?"

"We're better equipped for a battle of this magnitude this time. Our odds of victory are much higher now than they ever could've been before." Singer's eyes narrowed.

"Are you implying that you *knowingly* sent us to our deaths?"

"Everyone knew what the odds were. Don't act like you're a voice for the dead now." Before Singer could retort, Alastar cleared his throat, leaning forward to place his elbows on the table.

"Though you both have made excellent points, you're overlooking one major detail." He turned his gaze to Bellatrix who nodded in agreement. Turning to Dove, Bellatrix's eyes softened.

"Any plan combining the dark and light faye will ultimately fail."

What?

"How is that possible?" The weight of all of their eyes scared me, but it didn't deter me from questioning them on it.

Singer can mock me all he wants later- I still owe him a beating for what he did to Ricky anyway.

"Can't you guys, like, make them do whatever you want?"

"Well, my dear" Alastar began, an amused smirk on his face, "light and dark are polar opposites. When there's an influx of light, the dark is destroyed. When darkness spreads, light dissipates. That applies to our respective subjects as well. Mixing them together will ultimately end up causing more harm than good."

"Oh..." I turned away from his intimidating gaze.

Now I understand what Jin and Singer were talking about. He does radiate power.

"That's why," Bellatrix spoke, her eyes moving between everyone in the room, "any plan we enact must focus on the strengths that each faye has to offer and exploit it in strategic battle plans.

Anything less simply won't work."

"In that case, we should leave the dark faye to attack first since they'll most likely take out the most soldiers using the least amount of spells." Singer proposed.

"But what'll happen if they don't? What if Hawk's men decide to shoot first and they can't perform a defensive spell in time to protect themselves?" Dove's eyes zeroed in on Singer.

"Are you doubting my subjects?" Turning her gaze to Alastar, she gave him a curt bow.

"No. I'm simply taking into account their survival instincts. Once they're aware they're outmatched, how many of them do you think will still fight?" And on and on they went. The conversation got so heated that even Elah chimed in to Bellatrix's displeasure.

In the midst of the mayhem, a low rumble sounded next to me. Confused, I looked around but didn't see anything that could've caused it. Hearing it a second time, I glanced down only to find Aric's scarlet face with his free hand bawled into a fist pressed roughly against his stomach.

He's hungry.

Smiling at him, I gave his hand a squeeze.

No surprise there. He hasn't eaten anything in months.

Giving the other five occupants a quick glance, I gently tugged Aric towards the exit.

If I wait for them to finish then Ricky will starve.

Keeping Aric's hand in mine, I guided us skillfully through the camp to the mess hall. Once inside, I led us towards one of the long wooden dining tables. Settling down at the end of the nearest one, a male nymph walked over. Two steaming bowls of heavenly smelling food in his hands. Setting a bowl in front of each of us, he walked away once more, returning shortly after to hand us each a cup of water. With a final nod to each of us, he left.

"This looks great!" Aric exclaimed, snatching his spoon and shoveling food into his mouth.

"I bet." I giggled softly, sipping on my own soup.

I watched him from the corner of my eye as he practically inhaled his bowl. The same man wordlessly came over and handed him some more while taking his empty bowl. Aric happily scarfed it down with a look of pure ecstasy. Though it's good, it's far from the best we've had. Our mother cooked at a level far above this.

It's almost like he forgot what food tastes like.

I frowned, scanning over his features as he ate.

How much does he remember?

My mind drifted back to the conversation I had with Dove almost a month ago. When she transformed out of her pixie form, didn't she say that she couldn't remember much of her life before? *And didn't she say she couldn't remember how she died?*

Oh- please don't let him remember that night! Though I still have nightmares, I don't think I can handle seeing Aric's terrified little face. His eyes swollen from crying and his cheeks stained with tears.

He shouldn't have to remember something so horrible.

Something on my face must have tipped him off on what I was thinking. He set his spoon down with a small smile on his face.

"I don't remember much of what happened the night... the night I died." His eyebrows pinched together, a look of concentration covering his features. "The time I spent as a pixie is fuzzy too." Covering his hand with my own, I returned his smile.

"You don't have to tell me about it if you don't want to, Ricky."

"But I *do.*" Determination shined in his eyes. "I want to sort out my memories. Who'd be better to do that with than you?" *Ricky...*

Forcing back the tears, I gave his hand a light squeeze.

"Go ahead, Ricky." With one final smile to me, he turned his head away, a distant haze taking over his eyes.

"That night... I remember it was... storming outside." His face scrunched up in concentration. "I was going to go to your room... like I always did but... I decided not to." A deep frown marred his face. "I wanted to prove to mommy and daddy that I'm a big boy and that I wasn't afraid." Tilting his head back, he stared at the ceiling of the tent with unclear eyes.

"After that, I remember falling asleep. I was dreaming about wandering around in a forest with bright lights surrounding me. Sometimes... I could see this really pretty lady that would play with me and the others." He turned to me, the frown melting away. "Now I know she was Bellatrix." The frown suddenly appeared again, his eyes narrowing.

"After a while, I saw you again. You looked so... shocked to see me. I tried to talk to you, but you didn't understand me. When you turned away, I was scared that you were going to leave me, but somehow, I stayed with you from then on. The last thing I remember is watching that bad man about to hurt you again. Somehow, I knew I was strong enough to stop him- to make him leave you alone. The next thing I knew, I felt a pinch and then I was standing in front of him." The haze over his eyes dissipated as he stared into my eyes.

I couldn't help my slack jaw expression.

How can he remember so much when Dove couldn't? And did he really transform... just because he wanted to protect me?

Slowly, a smile etched onto my face. Launching forward, I wrapped my arms around him pulling him across the table and into my lap.

At least he doesn't remember any of the scary things that happened to him.

"You don't have to protect me, Ricky. From now on, I'll be the one looking after you." His body rumbled as he laughed. Pushing away, he smiled brightly up at me.

"But Jay, I like looking after you. It makes me feel like a big boy." I couldn't help it, I laughed loudly pulling him against me.

What am I going to do with him?

"You two are incredibly mushy with your bonding." Barely glancing up at Singer as he approached, I shot him a halfhearted glare before setting Aric back in his own chair.

Not even he can ruin my happiness right now.

"What do you want, you heartless fairy?" It wasn't until I fully faced him that I noticed the grim line on his face.

I don't like where this is going.

"The final battle is about to start." My heart dropped. Singer folded his arms across his chest, a barely visible smirk tilting the corner of his lips. "Silverlining- we won't have to sleep in those terrible cots anymore."

XV

Just as Singer said, our entire army was mobilizing. Everywhere I turned, there were squadrons of nomads, fairies and nymphs scrambling. Throughout all of this, however, I didn't see any of Alastar's faye. I mean, there are thousands of Bellatrix's from fairies, nymphs, and some other creature I don't know the name of.

Where is Alastar's army?

Speaking of which, where are the monarchs? More importantly, where do I take Aric?

Looking down at him, I can easily see how lost he is. His wide eyes watching as everyone swiftly prepared for this final stand. Several groups about a hundred strong were organizing into lines, various weapons in hand. Dove was amongst five leaders shouting directions and placing them in their positions. Another large group was focused on setting traps- magical and non-magical- along the pathway and around the perimeter where Hawk's army would come from. There were even a handful of others working on clearing the camp. From tearing down tents, putting out fires, and disposing of food scraps. It almost made me feel a little out of place, standing and gawking with Aric.

"What should we do, Jay?" Glancing down, something hit me.

Has Aric always been this small? The top of his head barely reaches my hip. Even his hand clasped in my own felt fragile.

He shouldn't be here.

"Shooters, get into your positions!" My eyes drifted towards Dove as she pointed towards the towering trees lining the path to the camp.

She must know where the children are supposed to go, right? "Dove!" her head snapped towards me, her eyes hard.

"What is it, Jayde?" she quickly asked, turning back to watch the army set up. Taking Aric's hand, I rushed towards her.

"Where are the children being kept?" She spared Aric a glance before turning back around. "Aric has to stay."

What!?

"You don't seriously believe that I'll let-"

"Jay?" a tug on my shirt brought my attention down to Aric. "I want to stay."

...*What?*

"Ricky-"

"I want to help you fight. I don't want to be a burden." He looked down, his eyes watering. "And I don't want to see any more people get hurt by the bad man."

Ricky...

Biting my lower lip, I glanced away from him. I don't want to see him get hurt- I *can't* let him get hurt trying to help. How can I send him out into a bloody war- especially one where the enemy is specifically trying to *kill* him?

Then again, won't he just go anyway?

"Fine." I sighed, kneeling to look Aric in the eye. "I'll let you stay," turning my head, I gave Dove a stern look, "but he has to stay away from the fighting." A smirk cracked her features.

"He may be tough, but he's not tough enough for something like that." A soft laugh left my lips as I stood.

"What do you want us to do?" She glanced around at the area that was now devoid of everything but a large standing army of faye wielding various weapons.

"Aric will help the alchemist support the ground army." She said, pointing towards a thick grouping of trees to the right of the path. Looking closely, I caught a glimpse of bodies moving. As if on cue, a woman with brown hair stepped from behind the wall of foliage, her eye focused solely on Aric. "This is Liberty- the head Alchemist of the nomads. She'll tell you what to do." Aric nodded firmly. With determination burning in his eyes, he moved past both of us and headed towards Liberty without a single faltering step.

When did he become so brave?

A smile flashed across my lips as I turned my eyes to Dove.

"What should I do?" She blinked at me with a look in her eyes that practically screamed 'you-can't-be-serious'. "You'll stay back and help the medical team."

...*Excuse me?*

"I won't stay back here when Aric is in the middle of-"

“Aric is in the middle of nothing.” Dove snapped back, her arms folded across her chest as she glared at me unimpressed.

“Besides, need I remind you what we’re fighting to prevent?”

Our deaths.

“Like I’d forget that.” I whispered, turning on my heels and walking to the medical tent in the back of camp.

It doesn’t matter where I am, one thing is true. After today, this will all be over.

***

An hour has gone by and nothing has happened. Everyone is in position and ready for anything that Hawk tries to throw at us, but where is he? The scouts said he was close by. He has twice the amount of artillery he had when we fought him the first two times.

Is he waiting for us to die from old age?

“Jayde?” Glancing over my shoulder, Charlotte walked towards me, a hard look in her eyes. “Don’t get lost in your thoughts.

I need you to be prepared.”

“I know that.” I murmured. She opened her mouth to say something, but a resounding bang cut her off. Everyone snapped their attention towards the sound only to see a barrage of fire balls raining down. The night sky was alight with their fury as they descended.

“Oh my-”

“Get a barrier up- now!” Immediately, the faye standing before us grouped together holding their hands to the sky. In a split second, a blanket of white light covered the air above us. Not even a second later, the fire balls hit the shield, exploding on impact causing a thick layer of smoke to incase the area.

“Attack!” with a monstrous battle cry, a horde of nearly two hundred men burst forward.

Before the fairies holding the barrier could react, the soldiers reached them, the fairies in the front row. The rest were just barely able to summon their weapons to defend themselves. A screech from above was the only warning before hundreds of harpies covered the sky blocking out the moonlight. One by one, they swooped down either snatching up the enemy only to drop them from fatal heights or cutting them down using their sharp talons and wings. The fight only lasted for five minutes as the last soldier hit the ground, landing in a mass of disfigured limbs. Looking at the fallen bodies, I could only see maybe three or four harpies amongst them.

If we had them on our side from the beginning, maybe we wouldn't have lost as many people as we did.

The ground rumbling beneath my feet brought me back to reality. Focusing on the tree line where the soldiers came from, a wave of men came running at us. My eyes widened as they rushed towards us like a tidal wave. There were easily three times as many soldiers as before, but Hawk has even more coming. Without missing a beat, the fairies still standing before us summoned their weapons ranging from axes, swords, lances, to maces. With a battle cry, they met the soldiers halfway.

The fairies swung their weapons, taking out as many of the soldiers as they could while blasting the rest with their magic. From the looks of how everything was going, it looks as if the soldiers anticipated this outcome, because with every person that fell, a new wave of a hundred men came forward. It was an endless masquerade of blood and bodies. Neither side willing to give up, nor is neither side willing to let the other gain the upper hand. After only three minutes of the fighting, there were over two thousands of Hawk's men swarming the fairies and there are still more coming. Not even the harpies could lower their numbers enough to make it an even playing field.

At one point, I saw Singer and Favian within the midst of the chaos. Neither of them looked the least bit fazed by the never-ending supply of soldiers coming at them. To be honest, they seemed to be having competition amongst themselves.

I expect nothing less from those two.

It looked like Singer was dancing the way he seamlessly blocked, dodged, parried, and slashed soldiers. It's amazing that he only had a few splashes of blood on him. On the other hand, Favian was downright terrifying.

The only way to tell he had a sword were the few times it flashed in the moonlight. He moved like a tornado- shredding and ripping anyone who crossed his path like they were a bug. I could've sworn I saw him take a bite out of several people.

Sometimes I forget his regular diet includes people.

"Hey- you stole my point!"

"If it could be stolen, was it yours in the first place?"

...they could pretend to take this a little more seriously.

Shaking my head, I scanned the sidelines in the direction that Aric is.

From what I could make out from between the trees, Aric was crouched down beside a large number of other fairies. He was holding something in his hands. I can hardly even see his face though, if I know him as well as I think I do, then it's more than likely frozen in horror and fear over what he's witnessing.

Pursing my lips together, I glanced at the other cluster of trees

to where Dove was with a large group of nomads and fairies.

Why isn't she helping- they're about to be overrun!

Even from this distance, I can see her eyes burning with an excited fire as she watched the events play out. She held her lance in a tight grip, her entire body tensed.

Is she… is she waiting for something?

Within the next twenty seconds, four things happened. From the trees, over six thousand soldiers jumped into the battle. Dove let out a shout signaling for her men of about five hundred to attack. The nomads and faye in the trees shot out volley after volley of arrows and bullets taking out as many soldiers as they could. Also, our men are getting *destroyed.* The bodies began to pile high. The injured faye that were lucky enough to be brought to the medical tent screamed in agony as they were forced to be treated without any medicinal aid. Those who weren't able to reach us met a cruel and brutal end by the hands of the soldiers and it kept getting worse.

"Now!" Snapping my head in Aric's direction, Liberty threw a glass vial of a green liquid into the chaos.

Not even seconds later, dozens of other bottles followed, breaking on contact with the ground. A light green mist encased the ground. Soldiers who were knocked down and inhaled it twitched violently before their limbs stiffened. In their paralyzed state, the faye easily took them out. A few vials that hit soldiers in the head immediately brought them to a standstill, saving some of the faye from death.

The battle continued on like this. There were only minute pauses between the artillery and the potions being thrown, but the effects they had were immediate. Though they helped, they made the battle far from even. At this rate, we won't last for another ten minutes.

Where are the monarchs?

The deafening sound of thunder overhead brought all fighting to a halt. Everyone stopped, their eyes on the sky as lightning danced amongst the black clouds. Suddenly, a black mass fell from clouds, a ball of lighting cackling above it. The speed at which it fell made seeing whatever it was nearly impossible. Seconds later, it hit the ground, smashing the ball of lighting against the ground. The deadly substance traveled along the forest floor electrocuting nearly five hundred soldiers that surrounded it.

Mockingly, it began to slowly rise from its crouched position, swinging a double-edged blade in a wide circle to its right hand.

When they stood to their full height, my jaw nearly dropped.

Al-Alastar?

He was dressed in pure black armor with a pearl white trim lining the joints. A chain linked chest plate covered his front while the rest of his armor was thinly cut but appeared impossible to pierce. The fairy king smirked as a hundred guards rushed at him. Holding up two fingers, he drew a triangle in the air.

"Remember who you raise your hand to." A ripple of black energy shot out from his body going straight through the soldiers.

They stopped moving, standing paralyzed in their spots before falling, one by one, to the ground. Letting out a bellowing laugh, Alastar spun his sword once more before lunging in the direction of more soldiers. Taking a firm hold of his sword, he swung it in a sweeping motion towards them. With a flash of dark light, the soldiers fell, a large slash covering the front of their bodies from where the light struck them.

Geeze- why does he even need an army?

A light flashed in my eyes from somewhere beside me. Turning in its direction, my eyes locked onto Bellatrix sprinting towards the battlefield, an elegantly crafted lance in her hands. Her usual attire was replaced with armor that was the color of white pearls with a black trim that covered the joints. A pure white translucent cape hung off her right shoulder leaving a mystical veil in her wake. Behind her, Apple, Cherry, and Fawn followed, each dressed in their own armor ranging from green, peach, and brown respectively.

The minute Bellatrix stepped foot into the field, she gripped her lance with both hands, holding it above her head. Leaping into the air, she swung it down in a striking motion. As it hit the ground, a massive trench appeared in the direction she swung it, crushing a group of almost a hundred guards that stood beneath its path. She stood up straight, aiming her lance in the direction of another group.

A ball of fire materialized within seconds. Without a word from Bellatrix, it shot out, trapping fifty soldiers in its wrath.

"Look who's showing off?" Alastar bellowed, cutting down almost thirty soldiers with a single swing of his sword.

"Please, Alastar. If anyone is showing off, it's you." Bellatrix laughed, swinging her lance diagonally, crushing a group of guards under an invisible force. A smirk appeared on Alastar's face as he watched her. My eyes widened as a hundred soldiers rushed Alastar from behind.

"Alastar, look out!" I shouted, tensing with the need to run forward.

If he even needs it.

The fairy king didn't move a muscle, the smirk on his face growing by the second. Just as the soldiers reached him, a large trench opened beneath them. It devoured them whole before it closed. Rising from the ground at the same moment was Elah.

She was wearing battle armor, but it didn't look half as extravagant or powerful as Alastar's and Bellatrix's. Hers was dark purple that appeared black when not in direct light. The trim was the color of her hair - dark purple. Twin battle axes lay in each of her hands, both with a black ribbon hanging from their handles that held the image of two feathers conjoined at the tip. Her glowing ice green eyes gazed around the field before they settled on Alastar.

"I was wondering when you would come out of your little observation spot. Were you hoping to watch me or Bellatrix die?" Alastar teased, slowly turning towards her. A sneer formed on Elah's face as she slashed a soldier without even looking.

"As if something like this would be enough to kill the both of you."

"If you two are done, then I would suggest you get back to decimating these puppets." Bellatrix grunted, spinning her lance in front of her body blocking the barrage of bullets flying towards her.

Launching herself into the sky, her lance charging with a white light. A second later, she plummeted, stabbing her lance into the ground. The Earth gave a groan before a shock wave of magic forced it to convulse. It stilled for only a moment before the ground began to break apart. Soldiers tried their best to avoid falling into the cracks or dodge the debris that flew into the air, but none of them within the impact zone were lucky. The moment the ground stilled, Bellatrix was racing towards another group, taking out dozens of them at a time.

Alastar and Elah weren't slacking in comparison either.

Alastar hurls lightning and hordes of balls covered in black fire at the soldiers followed by strikes from his sword that devastated the land. Elah, on the other hand, was like a deadly tornado as she seemed to dance amongst the soldiers leaving a trail of bodies behind her. *They're so strong.*

The faye present were still fighting, but they looked like children compared to the power of the monarchs. Singer even looked pretty pathetic when fighting next to Alastar. Though he is very powerful, Singer simply can't compete with the overwhelming strength that radiated from the monarchs. For each soldier that Singer takes down, Alastar takes out sixty more- and Singer is taking out the most soldiers of the faye.

If they are this powerful, then what did they need to summon their armies for?

"Even though they're the strongest beings in the world," my head snapped to the side as Favian dropped from the sky next to me, "they don't have eyes in the back of their head."

"What does that have to do-?"

"Meaning," he started giving me a hard look, "even with all of their powers, if you and your brother were to die when they weren't watching, then it wouldn't mean anything. No one, no matter who they are, can resist the power of the jewel at its full potency. How do you think your ancestor was able to get the queen to grant him a second wish?" I swallowed hard, lowering my gaze slightly. With that kind of power, someone can control the world or completely destroy it. The sound of something liquid hitting the ground brought my attention back to Favian. My eyes were immediately drawn to the black mass slung over his shoulders. Puddles of violet blood formed below it, a club lying forgotten on the ground.

"Why didn't you tell me you have an injured man with you?" I shouted quickly taking the body from him while simultaneously calling over help to get him to a bed.

"One would think that would have been the first thing you noticed. You are working with the medics." I shot him a glare as two of the others came and helped me get him to a cot. He was bleeding heavily from his stomach from a deep puncture wound.

"He needs a doctor that can use magic if he's to survive." One of the men started quickly before shouting over his shoulder. Not even a second later, the doctor was by their side working on the patient. I let out a breath taking a step away as the doctor expertly took over.

"You seem to be doing well here. Keep up the good work."

Slowly, I turned to look at Favian.

"I haven't done anything-"

"You haven't died either. Since that is what all of this is about, I say you deserve some recognition." With a small smirk on his lips, he shot into the sky. Fluttering his wings for only a second, he rejoined the other harpies hovering over the battle, occasionally diving down to pick off a soldier or help someone.

They're all so amazing.

A minute passed by and around five more faye were brought to the medic tent in serious need of treatment. With my nonexistent medical training, all I could do was take them to the others and watch the battle.

A battle that is getting worse by the second.

Even with the monarch's appearance, the soldiers were still pouring in from the forest. It's like Hawk brought a quarter of the population of Clearapal.

How many families has this war ruined?

My heart squeezed at the thought. No matter how much I wanted to avoid it, those who have nothing to do with this will lose the most.

All because of a stupid jewel.

A loud whistle brought me out of my musings. Scanning the battlefield for the source, Alastar's grinning face caught my attention. Not even three seconds later, the ground began to shake violently in a frightening familiar way.

No way…

Turning towards the trees behind us, it only took a second before the dreaded sight of over two hundred ogres, hobbes, and goblins bursted out. They stampeded right into the battlefield cutting down hundreds of soldiers and they didn't stop there.

The ogres smashed and stomped all that crossed their path easily. Hobbes and Goblins went toe to toe with the enemy using their oversized, crude weapons to tear them to shreds. All in all, the scene is something I *never* want to experience again. It's a bloody massacre - something Aric shouldn't be witnessing for any reason.

Though I hope he's only focusing on throwing those vials.

Swallowing hard, I glanced over in his direction.

Thankfully, it seems like his job was reduced to handing out vials to the older faye. They looked to be trying to strategically hit certain soldiers to aid their comrades.

I guess allowing a little boy to blindly throw potions wasn't a good idea.

I grunted, scanning the battlefield. The more I saw, the more a sinking feeling settled in my gut.

It was like Hawk brought all the soldiers in Clearapal the way they kept pouring in. All of them held that same fog in their eyes , blinding them from their instincts. I doubt any of them would willingly be here after seeing the way their comrades were being slaughtered. Even still, they kept swarming. However, something doesn't feel right about this.

Why hasn't Hawk shown up? Why isn't he making an appearance to terrify me or even threaten Aric?

Where is he?

"Looking for something, darling?" My blood ran cold.

Speak of the devil...

Slowly turning to my left, Hawk stood before me, in all of his glory, wielding a shining silver pistol in his sickly pale hand. A crazed smirk formed on his face as he took a small step towards me. "I've been looking for you." If it was even possible, he looked *worse* from the last time I saw him.

His eyes were hollow and surrounded in black circles. From his lack of armor, it's obvious how much weight he lost from the way his bones stuck out. The hair on his head had thinned even more to the point the bold spots became more apparent. Not to mention his skin held a deathly pallor to it. I swallowed hard, trying my best to contain the fear that threatened to consume me at the sight of him.

I almost feel bad for him.

"I must say," he started. Even his voice lost its smooth tenor and poised edge. Now, he sounded like a man on the verge of keeling over and dying. "You are *unbelievably* hard to get a hold of. Although, I guess that doesn't matter now. No one is going to save you and that little brat." A glint filled his eyes as he raised the gun towards me. "I wonder, how does it feel to stare death in the face for a second time?" he laughed.

My heart pounded in my ears. My blood burned as it pulsed through me, filling me with a burst of energy I've never felt before. My muscles tensed involuntarily, my brain racing a mile a minute. He says he's going to kill me again. He says after he kills me he's going to kill Aric *again.*

I'll kill us both before I let him touch Ricky!

Just like that, something in my mind snapped into place. My body moved on its own accord, diving to the side as he pulled the trigger. The bullet that would have claimed my life whizzed past my face, barely grazing my cheek in the process. Rolling to a stop, my wild eyes searched around me for anything to use to defend myself with. The sight of the injured harpy's club caught my eye, still lying on the ground next to the drying splotches of violet. Snatching it, I shot to my feet, racing towards Hawk with a battle cry as he glaring menacingly at me.

"I won't let you touch my brother!" I screamed, swinging the weapon as hard as I could at his head.

Without showing a single sign of discomfort, he raised a hand, grabbing it effortlessly. Letting out an animalistic growl, he roughly yanked the club from my grasp. Holding it firmly, he slammed it against my side, knocking me to the dirt. Landing with a harsh thud, I wheezed desperately to get my breath back.

I have to get up- I have to protect Ricky and the others!

Getting a semblance of control over myself, I slowly crawled to my knees. Before I could gain my footing, a crushing weight settled on my back, forcing me back down. A groan ripped through my throat as shocks of pain shot through my system. My eyes watered as dirt and debris assaulted my vision, the urge to rub them nearly unbearable.

"You won't cost me ultimate power!" He screeched down at me, the horrifying familiar sound of a gun cocking filled my ears.

No!

Tears welled in my eyes as I thrashed and squirmed furiously. He just increased the pressure bringing a pained gasp from my lips as more tears fell.

I can't- I can't die here! I can't let everyone down- I can't- I can't- I can't!

"Goodbye-" he let out a muffled grunt as the weight on my back disappeared all at once. A gasp of relief filled me as I quickly scrambled to my knees to see what happened. My eyes widened in absolute shock and horror.

"I won't let you hurt my sister anymore, you monster!" Aric screamed. His little fist furiously flew at Hawk, but he easily blocked them with his forearms.

"Ricky- get out of here!" I screamed, shakily getting to my feet. Before I could fully get up, Hawk gave a viscous snarl, smacking Aric to the side. Aric grunted in pain but was snatched up by his collar. Hawk held him close to his face, his hands rising to squeeze around his neck.

"I'll kill you as many times as I have to!"

No!

I lunged to one of the operating tables and snatched a knife from it. Rushing at Hawk's back, I plunged it deep within his back. Hawk gasped loudly, immediately dropping Aric, his face regaining its color.

Spinning on his heels, Hawk shoved me away before staggering backwards. Aric, though coughing and spluttering for air, quickly rolled out of his path. Hawk continued to stumble around, his hands blindly reaching behind him to find the blade still buried inside of his back. Grinding my teeth, I snatched another, running at him with full force, and shoved it right in the middle of his chest. A cry left his lips as he gave one final heave before he fell to his knees.

His body keeled over, his hands gripping the scalpel in his chest tightly. As he did, the glint of a black chain glinted from beneath his collar before a small pendant fell from the confines of his shirt.

It was beautiful. A tear drop shaped moonstone- no bigger than a coin- that dazzled a brilliant dark purple with specs of blue, white, and pink that twinkled like stars.

Is that the jewel?

Not wanting to take any chances, I quickly reached down and snatched it from his neck.

Immediately, he punched me in the stomach before shoving me to the ground. I rolled before sliding to a stop. My stomach ached as I slowly rose to a sitting position.

"Jay!" Aric yelled, crawling to me. I didn't have time to respond to him as Hawk let out a mortified screech, his crazed eyes never leaving the jewel I clutched within my grasp.

"No! It's mine- It's mine!" he screamed shooting to his feet. Gripping the knife in his chest, he roughly yanked it out. He didn't even flinch as blood poured from his chest. "Give it back! Give it back to me!" he screeched, rushing at me, the knife glinting in the moonlight and a trail of scarlet following him. Taking a deep breath, the sight of Hawk's gun only a foot away from me caught my eye. Not wasting a moment, I grabbed it, getting to my feet. Shakily, I pointed it at his approaching figure. Gripping the jewel tightly in my hand, a wave of power filled me.

"Disappear!" I screamed before pulling the trigger. The recoil knocked the breath out of me, causing me to stumble a little, but I kept my eyes on Hawk. The bullet slammed into his chest, halting him in his tracks. He gasped, falling to his knees. He stared down at the blood gushing out of both of his wounds before his eyes slowly dragged to meet mine. I gasped in horror as the whites of his eyes turned a bloody scarlet.

"But... it's mine..." he whispered, falling forward. His body hit the ground with a soft thud.

He shook for a moment as a wet cough left his lips, but in the next second, he stopped moving with a fail heave of his chest.

He's... dead.

A sharp breath left my lips, the gun slipping from my grasp. At the same time, a soft breeze swept through. The moment it came into contact with Hawk's body, it completely disintegrated, blowing away in the wind without a single trace.

The blood that's been pumping vigorously through my veins finally began to calm. The sounds of the battle raging on not even fifteen feet away finally registered in my brain as I shakily turned towards it. Just as I did, the soldiers that came with Hawk froze. Their weapons slipped from their hands as they all fell, one by one, to their knees, breathing harshly.

Bellatrix and Alastar were the first to notice as they commanded their armies to stop. Without wasting much time, they both held two fingers in the air and drew a circle followed by a diagonal line in the air. A bright light covered the soldiers and in a second, it was gone. All of the soldiers were missing when it dissipated. The only sign that proved they were there in the first place was the bodies of those who had fallen in battle still littering the ground.

"It's over..." I whispered. My knees went weak causing me to collapse to the ground.

"Jay!" Aric cried, placing his small hands on my shoulders. "Jay, are you okay?" Glancing up at him, I couldn't help the tears that fell uncontrollably down my cheeks. Wrapping my arms around his neck, I pulled him as close to me as I could and cried.

It's over... It's all over.

XVI

Bellatrix and Alastar immediately began organizing the cleanup. Elah was sent to escort the dark faye back to their respective homes before day broke by Alastar. She didn't look too happy, but she did as she was told regardless. The rest of the faye- light and dark fairies, harpies and the nomads alike- began clearing the mounds of bodies. Both kinds of faye casted fire spells to burn the bodies. Surprisingly, the area wasn't filled with smoke or the scent of burning flesh. To be honest, it just smelt... clean. It's like someone had just raised a veil of death and despair that covered us giving everyone the chance to finally breathe.

I took a deep breath, squeezing Aric's hand, my head resting on his shoulder. He didn't say anything. He just sat next to me, his eyes watching the cleaning operation with a slight frown.

"Jayde." I blinked, slowly lifting my head from Aric's shoulder. Dove stood before us, the faintest sign of a smile on her face. "You did well today."

Really? What good has my existence done for those innocent soldiers who had no control of their minds? For the families that are left with a missing link? What about the families who will never know *why* their loved ones won't come home?

Then again, wouldn't it have been worse if I had died and

Hawk had lived?

I squeezed my eyes shut tightly, giving her a curt nod. Taking in a deep breath, I slowly opened my eyes. A sympathetic look passed over her features before she shook her head, placing a hand on her hip.

"There's no time to wallow in self-pity, Jayde. You have to take care of Aric and keep that fairy you call a friend in line." I couldn't stop the corner of my lips from lilting upwards.

Maybe I've finally lost my mind.

"Thank you, Dove." She scoffed softly, rubbing a hand across the back of her neck.

"Well then, I have to escort the nomads back home." She closed the distance between us, placing a hand on both Aric and my shoulder. "I'll see you two again soon."

Hopefully it won't be because of another war brewing.

I managed a soft smile while Aric grinned widely wrapping his arms around her torso.

"See you later, Dove!" She returned his sentiments with a pat on the shoulder and the slightest upturn of her lips. With one final wave, she turned on her heels and marched towards the group of nomads standing to the side of the clearing.

All of them looked worn, tired, and overall defeated. Even though we won, it didn't quite feel that way. Yes- we stopped Hawk from gaining the full power of the jewel, but we did at the expense of thousands upon thousands of lives.

What's the point of victory when there's no one around to celebrate it?

Swallowing hard, I turned back to face Aric who was still happily waving Dove off. As he did, I could clearly see the handprints around his neck along with bruises along his arm. All of them were turning a nasty black and blue. They looked painful, but from the way he was acting, you would be inclined to think otherwise.

He shouldn't have gotten them in the first place.

"Ricky, do your wounds hurt?" He paused, confusion painting his features as he turned to look at me. As if reading my mind, he glanced down at his arms before shooting me a happy smile.

"They don't bother me, Jay!" A smile formed on my lips.

Of course they don't.

Scooping him into my arms, I rose to my feet making my way to an unoccupied medical cot. Setting him down on it, I turned away from him long enough to grab a bottle of salve, gauze, and a pair of scissors. After dropping them on the bed next to him, I noticed his curious eyes zeroed in on the supplies.

"What's wrong Aric?" His gaze shifted to me, the confusion still clear on his face.

"When did you learn how to use medical stuff, Jay?"

So that's what has him so confused.

"I've seen the doctors and nurses patch up so many people I could do this with my eyes closed." I joked, grabbing the bottle of ointment and rubbing it along the bruises on his arms.

We sat in relative silence as I worked on massaging the soothing ointment into his wounds. The sound of the faye working was the only thing that broke the quiet that settled over us.

It's a blessing to have this tranquility after so much destruction.

After wrapping his arms in bandages, I moved to his neck. Our eyes connected for a moment as I did, and that's when I noticed something hidden within those depths.

"Do you have something you want to tell me, Ricky?" I softly asked, placing a generous amount of the ointment onto my fingers and rubbing it onto his neck. He didn't speak for a long time, as he just watched me.

"Are you okay, Jay?" he finally asked as I finished putting the ointment on. Faltering slightly, I gave him a small smile as I reached for the bandages to wrap around his neck.

"I'm fine and it's all thanks to you, Ricky." I smiled at him, tying off the bandages. Dropping my hands, I gave him a bright smile.

A soft blush touched his cheeks, his eyes widened with excitement.

"You were awesome, Jay! When that bad man was coming after you, you were like bam- and- wha pow- and- 'you aren't going to get away with that!'- you're so cool, Jay!" he rambled flailing his arms around. I couldn't help but laugh, shaking my head softly at his antics.

He's the same as always no matter what horrors he's been through.

"Ricky," he paused, the awe in his eyes never vanishing. "You shouldn't have been there- you shouldn't have been anywhere near here." The smile on his face only grew, his eyes softening drastically.

Shaking his head, he lowered his eyes to look directly into my own.

"I wish... I wish I was stronger. If I were, then you wouldn't ever have to see those horrible things again." My jaw nearly hit the ground as his words left me floored.

Isn't this supposed to be the other way around?

A soft smile covered my lips as I wrapped my arms around his smaller frame, pulling him close to me.

"It's not your job to protect me, Ricky. It's my job to look after you- and I won't let anything bad happen to you again." He tried to respond, but it came out as muffled garble as his face was pressed into my shoulder. I laughed softly resting my head on the top of his. "I love you, Ricky." He softly pushed against me. I loosened my grip enough for him to look me in the eye. The smile on his face nearly blinded me.

"I love you too, Jay!"

"What a miracle." I couldn't help but smirk as I saw Singer's approaching figure, "You two saved the day without any grave injuries. This must be a monumental occasion." I grinned.

"I'm glad to see you're alive and well too, Singer." He scoffed, crossing his arms and turning his nose up.

"Please, stray. Those soldiers weren't even *close* to being a challenge."

"Is that why I had to save you from being blindsided multiple times?" Favian piped in, dropping smoothly from the sky next to us.

Singer grunted, haughtily turning away.

"I had everything under control. It's not my fault you're partially blind." Favian let out a soft chuckle.

"I think that ego of yours will kill you before Jayde does." Singer grunted in annoyance, but the soft smirk gave way to his true thoughts. Turning to me, Favian nodded. "Congratulations on regaining your lost brother and family heirloom. Given everything that's happened, that's quite a feat."

"Thank you." I whispered, returning his nod. He tilted hishead before humming softly.

"With that being said, I have to bid you three farewell. I have an estate to return to and sleep to catch up with."

"Yeah right." Singer scoffed, crossing his arms. Favian merely smirked, patting him on the shoulder.

"Tell Ms. Lilly I said hello." He slipped his hand off of his shoulder and took a step back. "Until next time." With that, he shot into the air with a powerful flap of his wings. Twirling, he joined in with the large brigade of harpies heading deeper into the forest.

I wonder when I'll see him again?

A smile made its way to my lips.

"Why are you making that hideous face, stray?" I shot Singer an exasperated look before rolling my eyes. He let out a fake cough. "Well, if you're going to look like that, then I should leave so I don't go blind." With that, he walked into the crowd of faye finishing up with rebuilding the land.

What a weird fairy.

"Ye've done a fine job, lass." Turning, my eyes landed on Jin's approaching figure.

When did he get here?

"Jin, what are you doing here?" The ever-present grin only widened as he placed his hands on his hips, raising his head higher. "Well lass, after fightin' them bloody soldiers on the high seas, even I need a rest from the big blue."

Fighting soldiers? Does that mean there were more of them coming?

Jin must have read my mind, because he let out a soft laugh before rubbing the back of his neck.

"It seems that nymph was right about there bein' more comin'. Ye should be lucky that we be able to sink so many of 'em.

Otherwise, ye would have had to deal with nearly two thousand more - not to mention the artillery they were carryin'."

"Thank you, Captain Jin." I smiled brightly at him to which he returned ten fold.

"No need fer that, lass." I let out a soft chuckle before a thought came to mind.

Could Parsley have been amongst the harpies?

"By the way," I started, lowering my head from his questioning gaze, "did you see Parsley?" I chanced a glance to his face only to find a soft, sad smile. He took a step closer, placing a hand on the top of my head.

"Let sleeping dogs be, lass." He took his hand off of my head moving it to ruffle Aric's locks eliciting a sound of disapproval from him.

"Hey- don't do that!" Jin let out a bellowing laugh withdrawing his hand.

"Be a good lad for ye'r sister. With the way she's been fightin', she'll be able to whip ya into shape if ya don't!" Aric's eyes widened for a second before a determined glint entered them.

"She won't have to!" Another laugh left the captain's lips.

"I like ye'r spirit lad!" Jin turned his attention back to me, a soft smile on his face. "I best be gettin' back to the seas before they begin to miss me. Until the next time we meet!" With that, he whirled on the balls of his feet and marched off towards a line of awaiting horses.

I have to go visit him sometime.

Allowing one final smile at his retreating form, I brought my attention to Aric.

"I wonder if Ms. Lilly will be happy to see you." I wondered out loud, absentmindedly smoothing his hair out. A confused frown covered his face as he watched me.

"Who's Ms. Lilly?" Before I could respond, a white and a black pixie drifted by us. Turning, we were greeted with the sight of all three monarchs standing before us. Though Bellatrix and Alastar appeared happy to see me, Elah looked as if she was about to be sick.

What's her problem?

"You did very well today, my dear Jayde." Bellatrix stood beside me wrapping her arms around me and Aric in a gentle embrace.

"Thank you." Her eyes dropped down to look into Aric's.

"And you made us all proud with your bravery." A deep blush covered his cheeks as he squirmed slightly in his seat.

"T-T-Thank you, your majesty." He stuttered in a quiet voice. Bellatrix merely giggled softly making the blush deepen on his cheeks.

"Speaking of fighting," Alastar spoke, taking a step forward as he crossed his arms over his chest, his head held high in the air. "Did you see my legendary skills?" I couldn't help the eye roll. He must have been expecting my reaction because he let out a loud laugh. "I told you that I'm powerful!"

Why does he remind me of a tamed version of Singer?

A smile formed on my face at the thought.

I wonder if Singer would be happy or mad at the comparison.

A loud scoff cut off my thoughts as all eyes turned to Elah. The scowl on her face was more apparent than ever as she glared down her nose at me.

"Were you at least able to get the jewel before the human died?"

The jewel...

I swallowed hard as I felt it give off an odd warmth from its place against my chest. So much has happened because of it. A lot of bad things happened to a lot of good people just because it exists.

Then again, how many lives has it saved?

Without it, my ancestors would have died- Aric and I would have died by Hawk for a second time.

"Yes, I was." Hesitating only for a second, I reached for the chain around my neck and pulled it out from beneath my blouse. When my eyes landed on it, I gasped in shock.

It wasn't the same dark purple it was when I took it from Hawk. Now, it's an enchanting white with specs of pink, blue, and purple within its depths.

Why did it change colors?

"It's beautiful." Elah breathed, taking a step closer.

Raising my gaze to look at her, my eyes widened at the obsessive glint in her eyes. Her hand slowly raised from her side as if to take it from me. She didn't seem to notice how Alastar shifted closer, ready to grab her if she got too close.

What's wrong with her?

Not wanting to keep the jewel in her line of sight, I quickly tucked it away.

The moment I did, Elah blinked before shooting me a nasty glare.

What's her problem now?

Narrowing my eyes at her, our glaring contest was interrupted by Bellatrix shifting slightly so her body blocked my view of Elah and vice versa.

"So, what do you want to do now, Jayde?" She asked, the white ring of her eyes sparkling in what I can only guess as anticipation. I opened my mouth to speak when the weight of her words suddenly hit me leaving me stumped.

What do I do now?

I mean, now that I have Aric, I'm going to have to find a safe place for us to live. Of course, Lilly will want us to stay with her, but we can't stay there forever. I'm human. It'll only take one wrong move for me to end up dead. How can I ask them to take care of me in a place I don't belong? Then there's the problem with the jewel.

I could give it to Bellatrix again, but didn't this all happen because someone found out that she had it? I could keep it, but I'm human. How will I be able to protect it when I can barely protect myself?

And how can I put Singer and his family at risk because of it?

"I don't know." I finally admitted, looking into her eyes. She smiled tilting her head to look at the sky.

"Whatever you wish to do, we will respect it."

Wish… wish…

My eyes widened. I haven't made a wish to Bellatrix yet! I can literally ask for anything in the world and she will grant it for me- and without any nasty side effects like Alastar did. Looking beside me, my eyes connected with Aric's.

Thinking over everything that's happened- everything that he's been through ever since that night, I know what I want. I know I've said it time and time again that I want to be stronger. I've said it countless times with different motives backing those words, but I haven't done anything to make it happen. On top of that, I have no way of achieving it. I mean, what can I do? I could train to become a better fighter, but even then, that probably won't be enough. Besides, how long would it take for me to make any progress? No, there's only one way for me to gain power and stay with Aric.

"What did you do now, stray?" Singer groaned, strolling towards us. Even though his words sounded like he didn't care, the way his eyes scanned over all three monarchs told a different story.

"I haven't done anything, but I'm finally going to make my wish to Bellatrix." Turning my gaze to the fairy queen, I smiled softly at the knowing look in her eyes.

"And what may that be, my darling?" Taking a deep breath, I leaned closer to her.

"I wish to become a fairy." She didn't look the slightest bit surprised by my words as her eyes closed.

"I see." A tiny gasp to my right told me that Aric was completely floored.

"Why would you want that?" I turned my gaze to look at him.

"Because I want to be able to protect you. I can't do that without power." His eyes widened, before a soft smile graced his lips.

"Okay." Turning back to Bellatrix, I opened my mouth to speak, but Singer piped in before I could.

"No, no- you can't do that- that's a horrible idea!" Raising a brow at him, I cocked my head to the side.

"And why not?"

"Because if you become a fairy, then I'll never be rid of you!" he hollered back, his face shrouded in the horrors that his overactive imagination came up with.

Drama queen.

Shaking my head, I turned away from him, my focus completely on Bellatrix.

"That's what I want." She closed her eyes, a smile still on her face.

"As you wish." With that, she opened her eyes and placed two fingers in the center of my forehead.

She pushed it slightly before a burning sensation began to spread from her fingers throughout my entire body. Her image shimmered before she completely disappeared in a flash of white.

Another flash of dark purple shined from behind her, but my mind didn't quite register it.

My body felt light as if I was floating. All around me was a consuming, blinding white light. It's as if I entered some kind of dream world where nothing bad can possibly happen. I felt... light- almost as if I *became* light. There's no way I can possibly make sense of it. There's nothing I can compare it to. The only thing that comes close is when I was wrapped in Bellatrix's arms.

It feels like magic.

A gentle pinch brought me from that place. My entire being was plunged into darkness as a surge of lightning coursed through my entire body. It's like everything that I felt in that dream world was suddenly injected into my body.

Just as quickly as it all happened, it ended. I could feel a soft breeze caress my body. It was like nature itself was trying to tell me that I was back in the real world.

If that's the case, then where was that?

I didn't have long to dwell on it as a nagging feeling filled me.

Squinting, I slowly peeled my eyes open, groaning at the fuzzy blobs that invaded my vision. Blinking a few times, the blobs cleared enough for me to see Singer and Aric's faces. Aric looked star struck as he stared at me in wonder. Singer, on the other hand, looked as if he was watching a horror show.

"What are you looking at?" Singer's eyes narrowed dangerously as he turned away.

"You just had to wish for something like that, huh? Do you enjoy being a thorn in my side?" Raising a brow at his back, I turned to Aric with a questioning look. His grin stretched from ear to ear as he quickly reached for a small mirror and held it out towards me.

Looking into it, I was floored.

My ears weren't the same round shape I've had all of my life. Now, they're elongated like Aric's and Singer's. My eyes changed to a dark grey that faded to a light purple. However, they have the same light blue specs as Aric's. Other than those major changes, I didn't look much different.

So, I guess this means I'm a fairy now.

A wicked smirk formed on my lips as I turned towards Singer.

"Do you think if I asked, Lily would let us live with you?" His back stiffened. He whirled around, a threatening glare on his face. "Don't. You. Dare!"

About the Author

J. Elaine Knight's love of writing began with a love of reading. Starting in the second grade, Knight was introduced to storybooks by her teacher, Ms. Marble. First falling in love with dinosaur and animal books, Knight was then introduced to fantasy stories. From then on, Knight has been enamored with creating her own stories. Once entering the seventh grade, Knight and her family moved to the United Kingdom where Knight took her first creative writing class. After going through the course and working closely with her teacher - Ms. Amber Ali - Knight moved from writing short stories to noveling. Since then, Knight has strived to hone her craft and work towards a fulfilling career as a writer. Now, with a Masters degree in Project Management, Knight is fully dedicated to developing the Until Dawn series.

www.ingramcontent.com/pod-product-compliance
Lightning Source LLC
LaVergne TN
LVHW050648100826
845148LV00011B/2030

* 9 7 9 8 9 5 0 0 7 2 3 2 1 *